FALLIN'
FOR A
TEXAS *Thug*

A NOVEL BY

VEE BRYANT

Royalty Publishing House is now accepting manuscripts from aspiring or experienced urban romance authors!

WHAT MAY PLACE YOU ABOVE THE REST:

Heroes who are the ultimate book bae: strong-willed, maybe a little rough around the edges but willing to risk it all for the woman he loves.

Heroines who are the ultimate match: the girl next door type, not perfect - has her faults but is still a decent person. One who is willing to risk it all for the man she loves.

The rest is up to you! Just be creative, think out of the box, keep it sexy and intriguing!

If you'd like to join the Royal family, send us the first 15K words (60 pages) of your completed manuscript to submissions@royaltypublish-inghouse.com

Synopsis

No one knows the benefit of hard work quite like Briana Kane. She went from being homeless to living in luxury and she doesn't plan on ever going back to the hard life. When she met Dex, a dope boy turned club owner, she not only found love but she found someone who didn't care about her past because he survived through his life struggles, too. They have an authentic love. Both are fighters and it's that similarity that brought the two together.

Only thing is when you date a Texas Thug you sign up for extra baggage that you didn't know was there. Dex decides that he's going to get revenge for Briana but in doing so, finds himself in a sticky situation leaving him to ultimately betray his love for her.

Briana's best friend Kymani has been going through a lot with her on and off boyfriend Mike. He's controlling, and worst of all, in the streets. His recklessness could cost him his relationship, but Kymani already has one foot out the door. She's just waiting for the ball to drop so she can leave him alone for good.

It's not easy loving a thug, and for these two women the roller coaster is just getting started.

I would like to dedicate this book to all the women that have dealt with rape or molestation in their lives. I want you to know that you're not alone. We love you and I pray for your strength. If you haven't spoken up about something that happened to you, do it.
-Love Vee Bryant

Acknowledgments

I would like to thank my girls Hydiea and Prenisha, they already know how proud I am of both of them. I love y'all so much. To my publisher, thank you for taking a chance on me. To my readers, thank you for sticking with me through all my books, y'all the truth for real. I'm happy that I'm able to make you guys happy and want to read my work. I'm doing this for my daughter Lyla J, she is literally my motivation for everything that I do. She will never know how many late nights I have to pull to make sure she doesn't have to worry about anything.

Prologue

*D*ear journal,

    Once upon a time, I got my heart broken by men that I thought I couldn't live without. Men that showed me loyalty and love at one point, men that I went against everything that was right for. I've had a hard life, that's no lie. I've been through things that no child, teen, or grown woman should ever go through. My story is complicated, my heart is made of gold. My body has been used and abused so many times that I can't keep count. My soul is cold.

The only thing I've ever wanted in life was somebody who would love and cherish me.

It's true what Boosie says, "We're living in our last days". I want to spend those days with a man that appreciates me and what I bring to the table. I want to start a family with that man. Ever since I was a teenager going through body and attitude changes, I just wanted somebody to be there and ask what was wrong with me.

Why couldn't I go outside with my friends? Why was my foster dad so over protective? Why did all my foster brothers have to stay away from me? I was treated like I had a disease that spread easily, but that wasn't it. My foster dad didn't want me getting close to any other boys because he was scared that I would give away what he told me belonged to him. I didn't have a childhood and now it's projecting into my adult days.

I don't trust anybody, if I do trust a man it's very limited because I feel like in the end all you get is your heart broken by placing it in the wrong hands. And that's what I did; I fell for the wrong thug, the wrong man, the wrong dope boy. I truly thought he was the one, I told myself he was non-stop day by day. All the time I spent with him, all the nights we held each other and told our deepest secrets. He knows things about me that not even my best friend knows.

So, I was surprised when I learned about his betrayal.

Here's the story of how I got my heart broken, let's start at the beginning, shall we?

The feeling of someone viciously shaking me made my eyes burst open and I jumped up when I saw that it was my best friend Kymani, I laid back down and just stared at her. She was standing over me with a frown on her face.

"Briana, I hate to have to do this, but I think it's time for you to go. You've been here for longer than you said you would be and I'm getting nothing but hassle because of you being here. I'm so sorry."

"So, you're putting me out when you know I have nowhere to go?"

"I'm sorry this is not how I want it to be. You know I love you. With Mike paying half the bills, he doesn't understand why you're here."

"You know if I had the money, I would help you out."

"I know that, but that's the issue. You don't have any money and it seems like you're not trying to do anything but lay on my couch."

"Wow! You know what? Maybe it is best if I go. I thought that you of all people would understand what I had been through, but I guess not. Not everybody has a man that's going to pay bills for them."

"And that's my fault?"

"It's your fault that after all this time you didn't say anything. You've been walking around here with a nasty ass attitude but wasn't woman enough to tell me. I hope Mike makes you happy because I'm done with you!" I snapped.

A few months ago, my whole world fell apart. I lost my apartment due to not having all the money to pay the rent. I was living hotel to hotel until I ran out of the lil' money that I did have because the rooms were so high, and I had to eat someway. When you're staying in a hotel it's not cheap. That's how I ended up moving in with Kymani. It wasn't my intention to be here as long as I have been, but I ended up losing my job because the commute always had me late and the boss just wasn't having it. She made it seem like it was okay that I was here, but if she wanted me gone then I was gon' go.

Without saying a word, I got off the beige couch that had burn marks and food stains on it and went into the small bathroom so that I could take a shower. Looking at myself in the mirror, I was disgusted. My hair was matted to my head, I had eye boogers in both of my eyes and dried up saliva on my cheeks.

I never thought that Kymani would do this to me, she was supposed to be my best friend and yet she was letting a man that beat her ass nonstop control what she did in her apartment. A place he barely stayed in. I was pissed off but what could I do about it? I couldn't try to fight her in her own apartment and I damn sure wasn't about to beg her to let me stay. I'm not going to stay anywhere I'm not wanted anymore.

"You have to do better Briana," I said to myself.

I hope she didn't think I felt good sleeping on her couch either. It was uncomfortable, but it was somewhere safe for me to sleep. I never thought that she would let a man come and tell her what to do but I guess some people are prone to letting others down.

Turning around, I cut the hot water on then stripped out of my clothes and stepped inside to take a quick shower. When I was done, I wrapped the plush white big towel around my breast, I picked up a pink brush and put my long jet-black hair into a neat bun on the top of my head. I was mixed with black and Mexican; that was the best thing I got from my parents whoever they were.

I was adopted at the age of eleven by a couple who had more kids that they had gotten from the state. It was all boys and I was the only girl, the father was a pervert. He watched me when I walked around the house. He always made nasty comments when his wife wasn't around, and he stayed touching me. I didn't say anything but that led up to him molesting me every time we were alone. Living with them was okay if I didn't have to go through that all the time, it was like Dade loved to see me fight him off every time he snuck into my bedroom and undressed me. The last time he did that, I was fifteen and decided to run away. I couldn't take it anymore. My mind was gone and so fucked up that I didn't know what else to do about it, and I never reported it.

Pulling the door open, I walked across the hall and into Kymani's bedroom where my clothes were in her closet. Bending down, I rummaged through my things and pulled out some blue jean booty shorts that were guaranteed to have my ass hanging out and a cropped top. After getting dressed, I slid my feet into some black sandals then stuffed the rest of my clothes back into the bag and flung it on my shoulder.

I slowly walked out of the bedroom and back into the living room, Kymani was now sitting on the couch with a blunt in her hand, "Thanks for letting me crash as long as I did."

"You don't have to thank me, I'm sorry that I have to do this."

"It's fine. Can you hand me my phone?" She did and I headed for the door. I wasn't mad about her telling me that I had to leave.

Mike never liked me, but it got worse when I wouldn't fuck him. He just didn't understand that I didn't get down like that. I would never fuck my friend's man. When I told Kymani about it, she thought I was lying about the whole situation and was trying to make her break up with him, which I would never do.

Stepping into the piss smelling hallway of her apartment building, I strolled out of the building and was headed to my car when men started yelling and whistling at me. If it was one thing I knew, I knew I was a beautiful woman. My brown eyes could capture anybody, and my smile could brighten up a room.

Strutting across the street to my car, I popped the trunk and threw my bags inside. Closing it, I went to the driver's door and pulled it open. Sitting down in the seat, I was about to close my door when a typical dope boy in baggy Levi's, a plain black shirt, and timberland boots grabbed it.

"What's up lil' mama?" he asked.

Ignoring his attempt to try to talk some more, I shut my door and turned my music up before driving off.

The drive there, I rapped along with City Girls on their latest song *Act Up*.

Real ass bitch give a fuck bout a nigga.

Big Birkin bag, hold five, six figures.

Stripes on my ass, so he call this pussy Tigger.

Fuckin on a scamming ass, rich ass nigga.

Swinging my car into the parking lot of the club, I got out and looked in my rear view mirror to make sure I looked decent.

Upon walking inside, I noticed some dudes sitting in one of the booths staring at me. Turning my head away from them, I went to the bar and sat down.

"What can I get for you?" a woman dressed in a gold glitter bra asked.

"Two shots of Patron."

Nodding her head, she put the cups down in front of me then poured the liquor in each one. Picking up one of the small glasses, I downed it then did the same with the other one. I was trying to get my body to relax for what I was about to do. Swirling around in the chair, I spotted a man dressed in a smoke gray suit and matching loafers walking over to me.

"Long day?" he asked sitting next to me and watching the dancer that was on the stage.

"No, building up the courage to ask for the owner."

"For what? You're far too pretty to be working in here," he inquired.

"Thanks, but I need this job."

"I'm Dex, the owner. Can you dance?" he asked eyeing me. When he got to my thighs he reached over and grabbed one.

"Yes."

"Come with me," he stood up and put his hand out. Grabbing it, I let him lead me through the club and up some stairs into an office.

"So, do I just dance?" I asked, confused.

He nodded his head, leaned back in the chair, and put some music on. Beyoncé's song *Dance For You* blasted through the speakers and I looked down at him before rolling my hips to the beat. He moved his chair closer to me. Closing my eyes, I started to rub all over my breasts while dropping to my knees. The song changed and *Twerk* by the City Girls started to play.

I bounced and shook my ass while looking back at him, dropping into a split. He shook his head and bit down on his bottom lip. The song changed again and this time *Fucked On* by Plies and Lucci came on.

Say she ain't been fucked on in a minute.

Yeah, she says she love when I'm in it.

She say she ain't really made love in a minute,

Yeah, really made love in a minute.

Crawling to him, I put my hands on his knees and raised up. Turning my ass towards him, I sat down in his lap and started grinding on his already hard dick. I knew this couldn't have been professional, but the way he was looking at me while gripping my hips told me he didn't give a fuck. Getting back up, I faced him then straddled his lap. Bouncing slowly, I wrapped my arms around his neck and looked into his eyes. His dick got harder and harder with every bounce I gave him. I focused on the wall behind me and he had all kinds of pictures of himself up on it.

Finally, the song went off and I got off him, backing up until my back was touching the door.

He got up and walked closer to me. "You got the job," he smirked.

"I do?" I couldn't hide my excitement. It may not be the best job, but right now I'll take anything.

Hell yea, you're the first female to ever get my dick hard just by dancing," he laughed.

"Um, thanks I guess." We shared another laugh and I put my hand on the door knob. I was about to open it, but he grabbed my hand. He was looking into my eyes like he was trying to read my soul and my heart started jumping. Leaning down, he kissed me on the lips, and I put my hand on his chest and pushed back.

"I can't," I opened the door then ran out of the office.

When I got down stairs, I walked in the middle of the dance floor and out of the door. Getting into my car, I drove out of the parking lot and went to the nearest park so that I could get some sleep since I didn't have anywhere else to go. This was going to be my spot; nobody would ever fuck with me while I was back here. Gazing around, I locked my doors then closed my eyes.

Not being able to sleep, I started my car back up and went back to the club. I felt the need to tell Dex that the kiss he gave me was very unprofessional. I didn't need anything coming between me and my money. Right now that was the most important thing to me.

Pulling back into the club parking lot, I spotted him outside on his phone and parked. Jumping out of the car, I walked over to him and he hung up the phone. Sliding it back into his pocket, he looked at me.

"That kiss was out of line; I need this job so bad and I don't want anything to jeopardize me working here."

"Why do you need it so bad?"

"I'm homeless. I was staying with my friend, but she told me I had to go because her dude was getting tired of me being there."

"Damn, I had no clue. I have a place you can stay until you get on your feet and I'm not taking no for an answer. If you gon' work here, you need to understand that I look out for my people and you're my people now."

"Are you sure?"

"I'm sure, just because we shared a kiss don't mean we about to get married right now. I want you, I'm sure of that as well but I'm going to take it as slow as you want me to. Now, follow me to the crib," he walked off.

I watched as he got into a black Audi, then got back into my car and followed him out of the parking lot. Not even five minutes later, he pulled into a condo parking lot and parked his car. Doing the same, I got out of the car and he walked over to me.

"Why do you want me to live here? Do you let women you don't know stay in your Condo all the time?"

"No, I don't. I'm doing this because I see something in you, and I don't want somebody that works for me living on the streets. If they tell me their homeless and I can spare a room or anything I'll do it because God blessed with me this."

I felt myself blushing but quickly turned my head away from him. It's not often you meet a man who wanted to help you in anyway and he don't even know you. At this point, I was thinking he was heaven sent. Nodding my head, I followed him into the building and into an elevator.

When we got on, he pressed the button for the fifth floor, and we went up. He kept looking at me while I was trying not to engage in anything with him. I just needed somewhere to crash until I made enough money at the club to get my own place. The elevator finally stopped, we walked off and to a wooden door.

I watched as he put his key into the keyhole and pushed the door open. He stepped to the side, "Ladies first."

"Such a gentleman," I smiled at him then entered the house.

A black sectional sat in the living room facing a big ass flat screen TV that was mounted to the wall. He had white fur carpet and it made me wonder if he had a woman.

"I didn't decorate, I'm not a fur type of man," he laughed.

"I bet."

He then grabbed my hand and lead me through the three-bedroom, two bath place then back into the living room.

"I'll take the guest bedroom and you take the master. I'll be gone in the morning, but I'll leave the key that way you can get all your things."

"This is all my things," I pointed to my bag.

"You're kidding right?"

"Nope, material things don't excite me; they never did. When I lost my apartment, I had to leave everything behind because I couldn't take it with me."

"I'm sorry, I don't usually do this, but I'll loan you some money to get some things. Why do you want to be a stripper of all things?"

"I don't have a choice, I told you I needed the money."

"If it was up to me, you wouldn't even be working in the club. I meant it when I said you're too pretty to be taking off your clothes for money."

"Well, I need the money and job."

"How old are you?"

"Nineteen."

"Whoa, you're nineteen and trying to work in my club? Why not go to college? Where are your parents?"

He was starting to ask too many questions, but I started to answer them anyway. "I don't know who my parents are, I was put up for adoption at a young age and no college, I didn't even graduate high school. I was too far behind and I didn't want to repeat the twelfth grade, so I just said fuck it."

"No, you can't do that. You should go back to school, you don't have to actually sit in a classroom, you can do homeschool. Get your diploma and try to get into a good college."

"Why? So they can drown me in debt for the rest of my life?" I laughed. "I'm good," I added looking into his eyes. I didn't want him to think of me as some sort of charity case and the way he was looking back at me told me that's exactly what he was thinking about me. Shaking my head, I got up, grabbed my bag and went into the master bedroom.

Shutting the door behind me, I took off my shorts and shirt. When the door opened, he was staring at me through the mirror.

"My bad, why did you leave me out there?"

"Because you're looking at me like you take pity on me and I don't want anybody to take pity on me. I'm not handicapped, my life fell apart and I'm just trying to piece it back together."

"Well, let me help you find yourself again. You're so young and full of life, you should be experiencing it not stuck in Dallas, Texas being a stripper."

"We went from pity, to you judging me for wanting to be a stripper and make easy money when it's your club?"

"I'm not judging you at all baby girl, all I'm saying is work but don't get stuck in this lifestyle. I've seen a lot of girls come through my club and they still work there. You don't want to be taking off your clothes for the rest of your life."

That was one thing he was right about, I had no intentions of being a stripper for the rest of my life, but I also didn't ask him for his input.

"Look, I'm happy that you want something for me that I never wanted for myself, but that life isn't mine. I wasn't born to go to college or have fun."

"Lies, you can make your life what you want it to be. Hell, look at me: a dope boy turned club owner. I was in the streets when I was sixteen years old, I had to do that to help my mother pay bills and keep food on the table for me, my brother and two sisters. We didn't have a father and were struggling. I busted my ass and sold drugs until I had enough money and was old enough to open my own business."

"That's good for you. I just want to go to bed, if you don't mind," I said, and he got up.

He walked to the door then turned around and looked at me, "I'm rooting for you to be better than them other girls that work for me," he said then walked out of the room and shut the door behind him.

Laying in the bed, I pulled the cover over my head and just laid there until sleep took me over.

I was so worried about Briana and the fact that she wasn't answering my phone calls told me that she was mad at me. It's been about a week since I last saw or talked to her. I was scared that she had gone out and got herself into some trouble.

"You need to stop worrying about her. She's a grown ass woman that can take care of herself," Mike stated.

"I can't. I don't care if she's grown, I shouldn't have put her out," I was pacing back and forth calling her phone repeatedly, and it kept going to voicemail.

"So, you were willing to lose me all so that bitch could have somewhere to stay?" his voice boomed causing me to jump.

I didn't know what his problem was with Briana, but it was getting old and kind of Weird. I jumped on my friend about this man when she told me he tried to hit on her and now it seemed like I should have been questioning him.

"Do you have a thing for Briana?" I asked.

"What you talking about? I don't even like her ass so why the fuck would I have a thing for her?"

"Because I remember that time you was whispering all in her ear when she was drunk. You touched her on the thigh, and she pushed you away from her. You was so mad that you took it out on me."

"That was just a misunderstanding. We were both drunk and she came on to me."

"If she came on to you, why did she run away and why did you get so mad?"

"Kymani shut the fuck up! I don't want to talk about that shit! Come get back in the bed and let Briana do her!" he snapped.

Ignoring him, I grabbed my keys and bolted out of the house. Running out of my building, I jumped into my black Jeep and decided to drive around to see if I saw her car or something in the neighborhood. This is all my fault, I can't believe I let that nigga influence me and now I have no idea where my friend is.

My phone started to ring, and I looked at it thinking it was her finally calling me back, but it was Mike. Hitting the ignore button, I started to call Briana's phone again and it kept going to voicemail each time. Getting frustrated, I gripped my steering wheel and screamed as loud as I could. I'm guessing by the looks I was getting from the car next to me, it was pretty damn loud.

The light turned green and I went down the road when I saw a woman that looked like her getting into the car with Dex, the neighborhood bully. He was dangerous and ruthless to the point where I heard his own mother won't even talk to him.

Pulling into the parking lot of a strip that held all kinds of stores, I came to a stop right in front of his car so that he wouldn't be able to move without wrecking my shit. Hopping out, I walked over to the passenger side and there she was sitting with a smile on her face.

"Of all people, you're with him? I know I put you out, but you don't need to be with him."

"Calm down ma, she's in good hands," he cockily spoke with a smile on his egg-shaped face.

She put her hand on his arm and he turned his head away from me.

"Kymani, you made it perfectly clear when you let Mike come in between us that I had to leave. When I did, I left you and our friendship behind. So, why are you worried about me now?"

"I'm sorry. How many times do you want me to apologize?"

Her car door opened, and she got out, grabbed my arm, and lead me back to my car.

"You need to leave, I'm fine now. I have a job and I'm making good money."

"Working for the devil?"

"Kymani, you're the last person that should be calling anybody the devil when your boyfriend is still selling your own mother crack. You're dating the devil, why do you think every time he can't have his way, he beats your ass?"

"That's not true. Mike hasn't put his hands on me in a long time. You're delusional if you think Dex really cares about you."

"Okay, let me be delusional then. I'm grown and I don't need a babysitter."

"Don't come running to me when he breaks your heart."

"I won't," she smiled then got back in the car with him. As they drove by, he winked his eye at me and sped out of the parking lot. Shaking my head, I couldn't stop the tears that were running from my eyes.

Climbing back into my car, I headed back to the house.

When I pulled up, Mike was sitting outside on the sidewalk with a few of his homeboys until he saw me. He got up, walked to the car and yanked my door open.

"I told your ass to stop worrying about that grown ass woman!"

"Mike, I don't want to hear this shit right now. It's too much going on and I just want to be alone," I told him getting out of my car.

* * *

Heading into the house, I laid on the couch and grabbed the blunt that was sitting in the ashtray in front of me. Turning the volume to the TV up, I put it to my mouth and lit it. I haven't been this depressed since the last miscarriage I had. Yea me and Mike's relationship was up and down but at the end of the day he was the man that I love, and he love me as well. He just had a funny way of showing it.

Our good times outweighed our bad and that's why I stayed with him. I didn't care what Briana was saying about him being the devil. He may have had an evil side in the streets and sometimes he did bring his anger home with him, but I understood that. He didn't have me out there doing crash dummy shit just to get a hard on behind it. Dex was going to fuck her head up then she was going to come running back to me so that I could fix it for her, but this I can't fix.

If she continues to run with that man, she's going to regret it.

The door to the house finally opened and Mike walked in with Quez and Dreezy.

"What's up sis? You good?" Dreezy asked sitting on the couch next to me.

"No, but I'm going to be."

"Good. Mike told us what happened. Your girl is going to come back when she realizes that Dex ain't no good for her."

"When will that be? Huh? When she's locked up or dead?" I cried.

"Okay, stop thinking the worse. Go get in the bed and I'll be in there in a minute," Mike spoke.

Looking at him, I got off the couch and went to my bedroom. Shutting the door behind me, I threw myself on the bed and just laid there. Briana was young when I met her. She been living in Dallas her whole life and never seen any of it, so I took her under my wing and helped her out. I know I fucked up putting her out, but I couldn't take it back. I did what I had to do so that I wouldn't have to hear Mike's mouth and that was my mistake.

About thirty minutes later, the door opened, and Mike walked inside. "I'm going to head to Dex's strip club to see if I see Briana. If I do, I'm going to try to talk to her."

"All she's going to do is tell Dex that you're bothering her and he's going to kill you."

"I'm not worried about him doing anything to me. I can handle myself; I know what you're going through Kymani."

"You don't know what I'm going through, it's because of you I had to even put her out. Don't do anything, everything you touch you ruin!" I spat.

He looked at me like he wanted to kill me, but instead he walked out of the house and slammed the door behind him. Quickly leaping off the bed I went into the bathroom and took a shower. I was going to have to be the one to fix this shit.

When I got out, I dressed in a short black dress with some strapped heels. Looking into my mirror, I brushed my hair back into a low pony-tail then grabbed my keys. I proceeded to walk out of the house when I was stopped by Quez.

"Where do you think you're going?" he asked.

"Out."

"Oh, no you're not. Mike gave me strict instructions to make sure you didn't go anywhere. He said he's going to handle it and he don't want you anywhere near that club when he does."

"What is he going to do?"

"I don't know, he didn't tell me any of that, but you need to trust your man."

I didn't want to go back in the house, I also didn't have a choice. If Mike finds out I disobeyed him and tried to leave, he would beat my ass black and blue. He was controlling and that was one thing I found attractive about him when we first got together, but as the years went on it became worse.

Walking back through my door, I threw my keys down on the couch, stripped out of that dress and heels, then put them back into the closet. Sliding back under the covers, I decided it was just best if I waited until he came back to find out what happened.

The longer I laid in the bed, the more impatient I began to grow. I didn't know why I was so worried about Briana when it was apparent that she wasn't worried about me or my feelings. That was odd because she always listened to me, but that nigga had her so wrapped around his finger that she was ignoring her friend.

Not being able to keep my thoughts at bay, I rolled another blunt. Me and Briana always fought but this seemed like it was something different, like I was going to lose her for real and the friendship that we built and that was something I didn't want to happen.

My high was taking over, and I felt like I was floating on the clouds until somebody started knocking on the front door. Blowing smoke out of my mouth, I got out of the bed and went to it.

Without looking through the peephole, I opened it and a girl was standing there holding a small baby close to her chest. She had one of her hands on her hips and a mug on her face.

"Where is Mike?" she inquired.

"Not home. How can I help you?"

"You can keep his son until he gets here. I'm tired of keeping my child a secret while he runs around freely."

Putting my hands on my hips, I shook my head, "Excuse me? Whose baby?"

"Are you deaf? This is Mike's son. You're his sister so keep him."

"I'm not his fucking sister."

"I'm not going anywhere; I need to see Mike. He's not answering the phone, so I came here."

"And that's my problem why? I'm good but you're not coming in this apartment boo," I smiled.

She looked me up and down before strolling away with the baby in her arms. Shutting my door, I went into my bedroom and grabbed my phone, so that I could call Mike's no-good ass.

I didn't know where the fuck he was, but he needed to get here and explain this shit to me. His phone rang twice before he answered, "Hello?" his words slurring told me that he was drunk.

"You have a baby?"

"Girl, what you talking about?" he had the nerve to ask.

"The girl who has your son, the same girl you told I was your sister."

He got quiet for a minute, "I'm on my way," he said and hung up the phone.

Heading back into the living room I sat down and rolled me a blunt. I didn't even care to tell him that I sent that bitch on her way. He was gon' find out when he got here.

Thirty minutes later, he walked into the house with a bottle of Hennessey in his hand and was stumbling all over the place. "So, you had a baby on me?" I screamed not being able to hold my emotions in.

"It's not what you think, I didn't know she was pregnant."

"You a fucking lie! If you didn't know she was pregnant, she wouldn't have shown up here."

"Hold on," he said walking out of the house. When he came back, he had the girl and the baby with him. I shook my head, I didn't know what kind of family reunion shit he thought he was about to have, but he have me all the way fucked up. I've put up with too much of his shit and it was time for him to go. "Are you fucking crazy? I want her, you and that baby out of my house Mike."

"Watch your mouth."

"I want you gone. We don't have anything to talk about, I'm done with you and your shit."

"Shut up, we both know I'm not going anywhere. After everything we been through you gon' let this come in between us?"

"You're not the victim here, if you want to stay be my guest, but Kymani is out!" I stormed off and went into the bedroom. I was about to start packing my shit when I came to the realization that I wasn't about to let him run me out of my home. Putting the bag back down, I walked to the bedroom door. The girl was still sitting on the couch and he was holding the baby.

"You done tripping?" he asked.

"You need to leave."

"Kymani, I'm not going nowhere."

"I'm not asking." It was time that I got my life back starting with this toxic ass relationship. "I'm serious, I can't do this no more, I'm sick and tired of your shit," I added. I was scared of what he was going to do but at this moment I didn't give a fuck either.

Mike is the type of man that will do whatever he have to do until he gets what he wants. I can't help but think this whole situation was my fault, I let him get away with everything. Now, I have to fix it for myself.

He lifted himself up off the couch and walked close to my face, looking into my eyes he spoke, "I'm not going no motherfucking where! I pay the bills in this bitch," he spat.

That doesn't matter, and you don't pay all the bills just some."

"What the fuck did I just say?" he snarled.

The only thing I could do was nod, I wasn't about to stay around so if this meant me leaving my sanctuary then that's what I'm about to do. "Okay, you can stay here alone," I informed him before walking back into the room and slamming the door in his face.

Briana

$\mathcal{T}$he club was packed as usual and I wasn't doing anything except walking around with Dex. He was still showing me the ropes of how everything worked around here,

"Dex, what's up?" a guy that I had been seeing around at the club asked. He was looking at me with a smile on his face.

"What's up? Briana, this is Palõ. Palõ, Briana."

"Nice to finally meet you. I've heard so many nice things about you," he extended his hand and I took it. I looked up at him and immediately got lost in his hazel eyes, he had mocha skin and tattoos all over his neck and arms.

"You as well."

"Can I get a private dance?" he asked, and I turned my head to face Dex.

"I'll see you around," he said before disappearing into the crowd that was a few feet ahead of us.

Palõ grabbed my hand and together we walked to the back of the club.

When we got to the door that lead to the private dance section, he pulled me closer to his front. I was uncomfortable even though me and Dex weren't having sex. He was just helping me out as a friend. He never came on to me after what happened in his office.

Stepping into the red room, Palõ sat on the black couch that was in the middle of it and eyed me with nothing but lust. Turning around, I put on August Alaina's *Pornstar* and started to dance for him.

When I lay back, shawty don't know how to act

She ready when the lights go off, she climb on top

Her body rocking, we don't stop

No handle bars or falling off, cause

She ride me like a porn star

Climbing in his lap, I started to rock back and forward while his big hands gripped and slapped my ass. The way my eyes was rolling to the back of my head you would have thought we was fucking on one another.

Grabbing his arms, I put them in the air then turned my back towards him. While I was grinding and popping my ass up and down on his dick, the door opened and Dex walked in.

"Keep going," he encouraged me.

Biting down on my bottom lip, I looked up at him and started grabbing my breast then reached around to unsnap my bra. When it fell, Dex's eyes lit up and he licked his lips, I knew he wanted me just as bad as I wanted him. Palõ, who I forgot was in the room grabbed my breast and started flicking and pinching my nipple making me moan out. "Ooh."

When the song ended, I climbed off him and he handed me three stacks of hundred-dollar bills. "You got yourself a real money maker," he grinned and walked out of the room leaving me and Dex just staring at one another.

Leaning forward, I put my bra back on then stood up.

"I don't ever want to see another man touching you like that."

"You don't have to worry about that, it was uncomfortable," I admitted. To be honest, Dex was the only man I wanted to be touched by, but he's not showing any interest like he did the first time. Grabbing my hand, we walked out of the VIP room and headed to his office.

On the way there, I spotted a few of the dancers giving me the nastiest looks. I know that I was probably tripping thinking that Dex was really into me, but the feeling I got when we were together told me I wasn't.

When we entered his office, I sat all the money on the desk and waited for him to take his cut like he do with everyone else, but he just looked at me, "Put your money away," he insisted.

"Are you sure about that? Don't you think the other girls will be mad?"

"They don't know what's going on in here and I doubt you will say anything to them."

Nodding my head, I walked out of the office and walked across the dance floor to the back. When I got inside of the locker room, I sat in front of my mirror and started to remove the makeup and red wig that I was sporting.

"It must feel good when you fucking the boss," a very popular dancer named Winter spoke walking up behind me.

"Yea, you get to keep all of your money," her right-hand Barbie added.

I heard that Winter was messy, and she always fought in the club, I didn't understand why she still worked here, but when Dex explained to me that she bring in the most money I knew why he kept her around. I was trying my best to ignore both of them, until Winter decided she was going to sit on my counter top.

"Can you move please?"

"Aw, she have manners. You better move before she go get her man," Barbie joked.

"First of all, I'm not fucking Dex and secondly, if I was, I wouldn't mind letting it be known. Just leave me alone." I was so tired of these bitches; they been fucking with me since the first day I came into work and they didn't even know me. I told Dex that it was going to be a problem if they didn't stop. One thing about me is I didn't need Dex fighting my battles, I can handle that on my own.

"What you gon' do if we don't?" Winter asked touching my hair causing me to stand up. I knew if I swung on her they were going to jump me, but at this point I ain't give a fuck. I was about to show these bitches why I wasn't the one to be fucked with.

"Look, I'm not trying to fight so if you don't mind," I pushed passed her and the next thing I knew she had me by my hair and was trying to fling me on the floor.

Pushing her back, I punched her in the stomach making her grip on my hair loose. Raising up, I pushed her back into the lockers that was behind her.

"Bitch, get off her!" Barbie grimaced pulling my hair yet again. When she let me go, I walked closer to Winter and was about to go to work on her ass when Dex burst inside.

"What the fuck going on in here?" he asked putting his hand on my waist and pulling me behind him.

"We all see the way you treat her; the question is why does she get special treatment for fucking you when just a few days ago you was fucking me?" Winter blurted out.

Instead of standing there and listening to that bullshit, I stepped around Dex and grabbed my belongings. Storming out of the locker room, I let the door slam behind me,

"Briana!" he yelled my name and I kept moving as if I didn't hear a word he said.

Going up to his office, I was regretting driving with him to the club. Sitting down on the leather sofa I waited for him. He didn't have to explain anything to me although I didn't like the fact that he had me working with somebody that he fucked. That was the reason she was fucking with me which was lame because I wasn't fucking him.

"Why did you ignore me?" he questioned stepping into the office and shutting the door behind him.

"Because I don't think that girl really have an issue with me. She thought that we was fucking and that was her problem. She like you."

He sighed then sat in front of me in his chair, "'I know how that may look but I swear I didn't plan on fucking her. It just happened and I have regretted the shit since it happened. She keep blowing my phone up and stalking me."

"You don't have to explain anything to me. It is what it is, but if you get tempted and fuck other girls then you don't need me. You can have anybody you want."

"I know that, but I want you. Some shit just happened you know?"

I didn't even say anything. It would be different if I didn't know him, but he's a fine man that own a strip club full of bitches. Of course he's going to fuck them. I just wished he would have told me something before I started working and feeling him.

"Can I go home?"

"No, I have a few more things to handle then we can leave together."

I sighed and sat back on the couch, we stared at one another before he got up and went back around his desk. The entire time he was typing on his computer I was scrolling through my phone when a text message from Kymani popped up.

Kymani: Girl, I'm at Baby Dolls. can you come talk to me please?

I knew something had to be wrong for her to be at the club asking me to talk to her. I know that me ignoring her wasn't something she was used to, but I was pissed that she put me out of her home when she knew I had nowhere else to go. That was coldblooded and I would never do that to her. I don't want her to think that had anything to do with Dex because it didn't. It was Mike, I didn't like the way he did her and never spoke about it but the moment she seen that I was with Dex she just felt like she was obligated to tell me about myself.

Getting up, I grabbed the door knob and he looked at me, "Where you going?"

"My friend needs to talk to me and she's here. I'll be back," I walked out of the office and headed down the stairs. When I got to the bottom of them, I saw her sitting at the bar with a cup in her hand and headed over to her. "What's going on? If you here to tell me about Dex, save it please."

"I'm not here to say anything bad about Dex. I'm sorry about how everything went earlier I was just surprised to see you with him. You're so much better than him Bri and I just want you to realize that before getting swept away in his life."

"I'm not getting swept away in anything. I'm working for him and that's it. We're not even fucking around like that."

"I'm here about Mike, why this nigga have a whole family?"

"Fuck you mean, a whole family?"

"I mean he have a son with this girl, and he had her in my house. I tried to put him out, but he wouldn't leave so I left."

"Kymani, you can't let him drive you out of your own house. You've been putting up with Mike's shit for so long that you're okay with letting him make you leave. No, it's time that you put your foot down, he's not going to do you right and you know that."

She nodded her head and I grabbed her hand, "I love you and I just want you to be happy. Don't be like me. I been with Mike for so long and I thought that he really loved me, but it turns out that he just love having somebody to control and my dumb ass gave him that control over me."

"It's time for you to take your life back. You don't need a nigga to make you feel complete. That's what you got you for and me too," I smiled and hugged her.

"You here to start shit with me?" The sound of Dex's voice asking made me let her go.

"No, I'm not. I want my friend to be happy and if that's with you then I will respect it."

"Where your nigga at? I saw him walking around here earlier, my guess is he was looking for Briana."

"Maybe, I don't know why he was here. I was trying to figure out where his baby momma came from and the unknown baby that I had no clue about. Let me not forget about him telling her that I'm his sister."

"What the fuck?" I exclaimed.

"Girl, he had this girl thinking that I was his sister and shit. I couldn't even be mad at her because she was only going off what he said."

"That nigga got to be the most fucked up nigga in the world." Dex laughed and I joined in.

"Well, since you left your place where you gon' stay tonight?"

"I don't know, I might get a room for the week then hopefully he gets bored being at my house by himself and leave."

"I doubt it, he gon' find you and try to make you come back home."

"As long as he's there, I'm not going back."

"You can come stay at the house with Briana, they have an extra room and I'ma stay at my own house tonight," Dex offered.

"Are you sure about that? After all the shit I said about you?"

"It's nothing, not everybody knows the truth about me. They go by what they hear, and I've dealt with it my whole life but I'm not that nigga that people got everybody thinking I am."

I loved the way he explained that, especially when he didn't have to.

"I can vouch for that. He's amazing," I grinned so big that I was sure that she saw all thirty-two of my teeth. I don't know why I was so happy talking about him, but it wasn't a lie that he was amazing, and I was grateful for him.

"Babe, I'ma go handle the rest of what I need to handle including talking to Winter and Barbie about what they did in that locker room. You won't have to worry about that shit no more."

"It's fine, don't do anything that's gon' get me in no more shit. The last thing I need is for all the dancers around here to hate me more than they probably already do."

"Don't worry about that," he leaned in and kissed me on the cheek then walked away. Sitting down at the bar, I got me a drink and Kymani got a refill. We both just looked at the dancer that was on the pole and she was doing her thing. That was something I wanted to do but Dex would probably have a heart attack if I told him I wanted to take my clothes off every night.

"So, what you do here?" Kymani asked.

"Dance, but Dex always cut my nights short. I don't think he like the fact that I'm giving private dances above anything."

"What do he expect when he have somebody as fine as you working in here?"

I shrugged my shoulders, "I don't know but he's going to have to let me do my own thing. I don't want to be told what I can and cannot do. This is where the money is, and I love that I don't have to do much to make money."

"And he have you up in a place?"

"Yea, he found out that I was homeless, and he helped me out. He's really nice and I don't think it's anything I can do to ever repay him for what he has done for me. I really think he's misunderstood, and I wish that people knew the kind of man he really is."

"I feel you, I'm starting to think that everything I heard about him isn't true. I was going off what Mike told me, and he might have been saying that just because he don't like Dex. You know he and Dex used to be really tight until Dex took his money and opened clubs then he left the streets alone."

"I'm pretty sure Mike could have left the streets alone as well, he just love that fast money and going to jail," I joked and we both laughed.

Gazing up, I spotted Winter and Barbie going to Dex's office and I wanted to go up there so bad but decided to let him handle it the way he wanted to. I couldn't go in there and say anything because they bullied me all because of him. I know how to get bitches mad.

"Are those the dancers he was talking about?" Kymani asked.

"Yea, they tried to jump me in the locker room because Winter thought I was fucking Dex. I guess she's territorial behind a man that doesn't even want to be with her or have anything to do with her. He fucked up fucking her and now he have a monster on his hands."

"Damn."

I didn't even respond because she wasn't going to understand. I was so ready to go home so that I could take a shower, smoke, and get my ass in the bed.

"So, what you want to say about that shit you pulled Winter?" I interrogated. I was so tired of these bitches, they make everything hard and that's why I couldn't keep no dancers already, but they wasn't about to run Briana off. I like her, so I wanted her close to me.

"You need to get your nose out of her pussy. You know she'll never give you what I did."

"What's that?" I put my hand on my goatee and started stroking it with a grin on my face. "Pussy?"

"Don't play with my bitch, she gave you everything and you had her thinking that she had a chance to be with you only for you to come to the club with a new bitch and you expect us to work with her?" Barbie's ugly ass inquired.

"I'm not asking you to do anything, you can always quit. That's your problem, you always in other people's business. Winter is a grown ass woman and I highly doubt she need you to co-sign everything, and if she does then she's weaker than I thought."

"I'm far from a weak bitch and you know that, but if you knew that you was feeling somebody else you should have left me alone."

"I told you about her, me and her not even together and if we was it wouldn't be a secret. I want to make this the last time I have a conversation about either of you fucking with her, if you don't want to work with her then quit," I shooed them both away and watched as they exited my office.

That was the last thing I needed to handle, I wanted to spend some time with Briana, but I was going to let her take care of her friend. She had told me how Kymani was there for her when she needed her the most, but yet she was quick to put her out. I don't know what to think about that, but that's her friend and it wasn't shit I could say about it.

Standing from my desk, I turned my computer off and headed for the door. Pulling it open, I walked out and locked it behind me. I couldn't trust nobody in my office while I wasn't here so I made my manager her own office so that she could handle business while I was gone. I never stayed here all night and it wasn't about to start tonight.

"Aye, I'm about to head out."

"Okay, I can handle it for the next two hours."

"If Winter and Barbie start anymore shit let me know. Them bitches skating on thin ice with me."

"Got you boss. Have a good night with that fine girl you got here," she smiled causing me to chuckle.

"Not tonight Shala," I walked away from her and went back down the stairs. Her and Kymani were still sitting at the bar and she had another drink in her hand, "Let's go," I put my arm around her waist and helped her up.

Everybody was staring at us and with every step I took, niggas was mugging, and bitches was smiling. If I wanted, I could have had all these bitches walking around my mansion with no clothes on sucking dick and fucking all night, but Briana had a nigga wanting to act right. She was different from the bitches I'm used to. She was humble about her beauty and that's why I always felt the need to let her know that she was sexy as fuck.

"I'm so drunk," she purred. Shaking my head, I sat her in the passenger seat of my whip, buckled her in, and shut the door.

"Follow me," I told Kymani and she nodded her head then got into her car. Stepping around the car, I got into the driver side and started it. Driving out of the parking lot, we headed to the condo.

The entire ride, Briana was mumbling something in her sleep then she unbuckled her seatbelt and reached over the console. "Whoa! Chill out Bri," she grabbed my dick as hard as she could and usually that shit would be a turn on if she wasn't so drunk.

I don't fuck females while they're drunk because I want her to be in her right mind when I give her this dick.

"Why don't you want me?" she frowned.

"If you think that then you not ready for me. I'm not a lil' ass boy, I feel you a lot, so I don't want to just fuck you," I pushed her back in her seat and she put her hand on her head like I hurt her.

Pulling my car into the parking lot of the condo building, I parked close to the door so that I would be able to carry her inside. Getting out of the car, I went back over to her side and opened the door. Reaching down, I picked her up, shut the door with my foot, and took her inside of the building.

Kymani was right behind us and she was laughing, "Her ass is out of there."

"Facts, I think the shit that transpired between her and Winter got her feeling some type of way."

"What happened? You fucked her?"

"Who? Winter?"

She nodded her head, "I mean I may have fucked around with her a few times before I met Briana and one time after. I don't want her to let that get to her, I told her that I don't want Winter that was just something that happened."

"Do you realize that females think deep into everything? If you didn't let her know before you fucked her that you wasn't trying to wife her then she probably read into that."

"I let her know that I didn't want to be with her like that."

"Mhm."

Putting the key into the door, I unlocked it and pushed the door opened. Stepping inside I took her into the master bedroom and laid her down on the bed. Moving back, she was twisting and turning, and her arch was crazy beautiful. Leaning down, I pulled her tights off and she didn't have on any panties. Shaking my head, I put her under the covers and kissed her on the lips.

"Dex..." she moaned in her sleep.

"Good night Briana, I'll talk to you tomorrow," I spoke before walking out of the room and shutting the door.

Leaving out of the condo door and building, I got into my car and was about to drive off when my phone started to ring. Looking at it, I saw that it was my lil' sister Dulce and decided to answer, "Yea?"

"What you doing bro?"

"Shit, just brought Briana drunk ass home." My sister was the only one that knew about me and Briana. She knew how much I liked her but told me to take it slow because the last few bitches I fucked with was only fucking with me because of the money that a nigga gave them.

I wasn't hurt when the bitches got what they wanted and moved around because I was already doing me, they were just hoes that I could fuck whenever I wanted to. "You really like her, don't you?" she asked.

"I might, I don't like the fact that she get so drunk to the point that I have to carry her out of the club but I rather it be me than any of these other sick niggas. I'ma talk to her about that shit tomorrow, but what's up? You only call me when you want something."

"Shut up, no I don't but I do need some advice."

"Lay it on me."

"Okay, so I've been dating this older man and he wants me to move in with him and I said no. Now, we're in a big fight because I won't tell him yes."

"My advice is don't move in with no nigga and you already knew I was going to say that. You're in college and you're young all he want to do is control you and what you do. Don't be dumb Dulce."

"I know but I needed to hear you say it yourself so I would know I wasn't tripping. The last thing I want is to be tied down to a grown man whose already been married and have children. That's probably what he's used to but I'm not giving in that easy, if he's that pressed about me moving in then he can wait."

"Right, and if he have an issue with it tell him to hit up your big brother and I'll make sure he understands."

"Yo ass be ready," she laughed, and I joined in. She know I don't play when it comes to her or my other sister Rina.

We sat on the phone for the entire ride to my house, "Dulce, why you sitting on my phone?"

"I can't want to talk to my brother? You've been so busy that we barely see you, moms been asking about you."

"I don't know why she asking about me when she can call me herself and ask me anything she wants to know. It's crazy how she cut me off because of what I did for a living, but yet her boyfriend sells drugs."

"She blames you for Trayvion dying," Dulce reminded me.

Yea, you heard right. My own mother blamed me for everything that involved my brother Trayvion and the fact that he died on my watch didn't make anything better. "If she want to know anything, she can call me, don't tell her anything about me sis."

Pulling up to the house, I parked next to my other car then got out, "Well, I love you. Be careful and I can't wait to meet Briana when I get home for the break."

"I can't wait for you to meet her either, better hope we still fucking with each other. Bye." Hanging up the phone, I pushed the door open and went inside.

Walking further into the house, I went straight to my office so that I could go over the books for the club. I don't know why I went over this shit every day, I guess so that I could stay on top of my game just in case anybody ever needed to come in and look at them.

While I was sitting down, I started to notice that something wasn't right. I don't know if I was just tired or what, but it seemed as though somebody was stealing from me at least that's what the books indicate since my shit was five hundred dollars short. The only person that was handling money was my manager and I know she wasn't stealing from me. She couldn't have been when I went out on a limb to give her this job and teach her everything.

Sighing, I picked up my phone and called her, the phone rang twice before she answered, "Hello?" her soft voice spoke through the speaker.

"Hey, we need to talk about the books."

"What about them?"

"It's five-hundred-dollars short, is there anything you want to tell me?"

I asked. I was pissed but I didn't want to go off on her and the money was just misplaced or something.

She got quiet on the phone for a second and I could hear her crying, "I took it, I needed it for something, but I also just put it back. I'm so sorry."

Slamming my fist on the desk, I asked, "Why the fuck wouldn't you ask me for it? All that I do for you, to make sure you're good and you stealing from me?"

"Because you already do so much for me, I put the money back. All of it, I swear."

I couldn't even say anything, so I just hung up the phone. I hated that I had to do this to her, but I can't condone anybody stealing from me so tomorrow she was going to lose her job and I was going to have to get somebody in there who would never do no shit like that to me.

I put way too much money and time into my clubs for somebody to come in and think it's okay to steal from me. That shit wasn't going to fly with me. Tomorrow was going to be a long day and I wasn't prepared for this shit at all.

*T*he sun beaming in through the blinds of the bedroom made me put the cover over my face and stretch. I couldn't believe I let myself get wasted like a white girl yesterday, I don't even remember much that happened after that. Pulling the cover off my face, I was about to get up when I forgot I didn't have any panties on and shook my head. *How embarrassing.*

Sliding all the way off the bed, I went into the private bathroom that was in the master and looked at myself in the mirror trying to piece last night together. I don't know if I fucked Dex or not, but he wasn't even here for me to ask.

After handling my personal hygiene, I walked out of the restroom and got dressed in a blue jean dress and put my feet into some red Fenty slippers. I wasn't about to go anywhere right now but I at least wanted to be looking like something just in case. Opening the bedroom door, I stepped out and Kymani was in the living room smoking a blunt.

"Well, look who decided to wake up," she said looking over at me.

"Please tell me I didn't fuck Dex."

"He made sure you were good then left."

Shaking my head again, I grabbed my phone and started scrolling through my missed calls and he was the first one on the list. Hitting the call back button, I put the phone to my ear and waited for him to answer.

"Yo?"

"Hey, I'm sorry I got so drunk last night. I don't know what came over me but that's not me."

"It's good, what you up to right now? I have to head to the club, and I wanted to know if you wanted to come with me. I have to handle something, and I want you to be there."

I thought about it for a second, "I don't know, I feel like I've been involved in way too much already and the last thing I need is for people to start thinking that you letting me run your business."

"I know what you saying but this don't have anything to do with that. I want to spend some time with you."

"Okay, come get me since you just miss me so much," he started to chuckle, but he knew it was the truth and that's why he didn't say anything back. Dex and I always spend time together even if it's just us in the house. I didn't like going places that people might notice me from the club. He didn't like it but respected it.

Hanging up the phone, I went back into the bedroom and exchanged my slippers for some black and yellow Vans. Standing in front of the mirror, I grabbed a comb and parted my hair down the middle and proceeded to put my hair into two ninja buns on the top of my head.

Today was my day off, so I wanted to be as comfortable as possible. I hoped we wouldn't be at the club long today either, the last thing I needed was for anybody to be asking me to do something. I went back into the kitchen and fixed me a glass of orange juice and grabbed some bacon off the plate that Kymani had sitting on the stove for me and put it in my mouth.

Putting the cup up, I took a sip of it then my phone started to ring letting me know that Dex was outside, "I'll be back girl. Have fun," I told Kymani before walking out of the house. I was standing at the door waiting for the elevator to open, but it was taking too long so I took the stairs.

Stepping out of the building, he was sitting in his car in front of the building. "Good afternoon," I said opening the door and climbing inside of his Tahoe truck.

He looked at me with a smile on his face then leaned over and kissed me on the lips, "Good afternoon ma, how did you sleep?"

"Great, even though I woke up with no panties on."

"I didn't do anything but get you undressed. I would never fuck you while you out of there the way you was. The last thing I need is for a female to think I took advantage of them. I want you to remember this dick."

I couldn't help but laugh, I felt exactly where he was coming from. The last thing I wanted was for him to think that I was so drunk that I didn't remember. "I would never get that drunk again, I hate the feeling of waking up in the morning and not knowing what happened. I don't even remember how I got home."

"I took you of course, I wasn't about to let any other nigga even think they had the chance to fuck with you."

"Thank you for taking care of me, anybody else probably would have fucked me and I would have never remembered it," I turned my head and looked at him.

"How do you feel about me and you being together? Briana, I never thought I would feel this way about somebody I just met not too long ago. Your smile make me want to stare at you all the time, you're beautiful and it's not like I never seen a beautiful woman before, it's just that your beauty is drawing me in, and I want to know more about you."

"I want to be with you too, but I don't want it to seem like we're rushing anything. I want us both to be sure that this is something that we want. I have had a lot of hurt done to me in the past and that's something I never want to experience again."

"I do want this, I'm telling you that it's not another female that I would do any of this for. I don't fall for females like that, because all they want is money from a nigga like me. I really feel like you're going to be in my life for a long ass time and I hope that's something that you want as well," he let out. I could tell that this was something that he been having on his mind, but he had to make sure that he was having the same feelings as me.

Dex was a man that I wouldn't think would ever be ready to settle down, he had all kinds of things going on not to mention females always throwing pussy at him. I didn't want to be the girlfriend that had to worry about if my nigga was cheating on me or get confirmation that he was, so I was still going to take things slow with him. "I understand what you're saying but we still need to take things slow. I don't want us to rush things then you break my heart."

He reached over and grabbed my hand, intertwining our fingers, he looked at me, "I'm telling you that I won't break your heart, but we can continue to take things slow."

"I'm not saying that for sex though," I laughed, and he joined in.

"Good, because I've been dying to get inside of you. You spending the night with me tonight?"

"Don't you have to be at the club?"

"Nah, I'm thinking about closing the club for tonight. My manager stole some money from me, so I have to find another manager and make sure they know what they're doing before leaving them in charge of my club. I would rather worry about that Monday than now."

"Okay, so what we gon' do?"

"We can go out of town if you trust me enough to come with me."

"I trust you, but why do we have to go out of town? I want to make sure Kymani is good and stuff."

"She's grown, I think she can handle being alone at the house for the next few days. If you don't want to come with me that's all you have to say."

Dex didn't know how bad I did want to go with him out of town, but that would be the opposite of us taking things slow. I don't want to be pressured into having sex, even if it's something that I wanted.

"Of course, I'll go."

He nodded his head and continued the drive to the club. When we pulled up, he parked right in front of the door. Getting out of the car, he grabbed my hand and we walked inside.

The manager of the club was sitting at one of the chairs conversing with Winter and Barbie until they saw us then all I saw was eye and neck rolls. Those bitches were truly some haters and that wasn't healthy.

"You ready to have this conversation Shala?" he asked, and she nodded her head.

Moving to the side, he let Winter and Barbie get out of the way before I sat in one of the chairs and he sat next to me, "Before we start, why do she have to be here?"

"She's here because I brought her with me. I don't know what the fuck everybody problem is with Briana. Ever since she started working here y'all been up her ass," he snapped, and I rubbed his shoulder so that he could calm down.

"I didn't mean it like that, I don't have anything against her."

"Look, never mind all that. You know I appreciate everything you've done for this place and the fact that you close up for me every night. You make sure the dancers are good and they don't have anything to worry about, but the fact that you stole from me is really taunting me. I told you that it was one thing I didn't like and that was a thief."

"I put the money back."

"I know you did, but I can't condone you taking from the safe, so I have to let you go," he put his head down. I could see how this was really getting to him, he didn't want to have to let her go but her stealing was bad for business.

"I understand," she spoke putting her keys down on the table and getting up. I watched as she walked out of the building. Winter and Barbie came back down the stairs and they both looked at Dex like he had lost his mind.

"You really fired Shala when she was the only one keeping this place running?" Winter asked.

He started chuckling then stood up, "I want y'all to understand something and that is this is my place of business. I owned this business, I hired all of y'all including Shala, she knew what she was getting into when she started to work for me. When you bite the hand that feed you that mean you don't need to work here. If either of you have an issue with it, it ain't gon' be hard for me to replace y'all."

I didn't know why but I was starting to feel bad for them, it was like Dex was ready to fire everybody and he needed to think about that before his business goes down the drain and he loses all of his dancers. I didn't know anything about any of this shit, so I sat there quiet until he grabbed my hand and lead me to the door, "The club is closed for the weekend."

"Are you serious? Those are our biggest nights." Barbie said with disapproval in her voice.

"I can't find anybody to run this bitch while I'm out of town handling business so yea, we closed for the weekend." And with that we walked out of the building and got back into his car.

The entire ride to wherever we were headed was quiet. I wanted to say something, but I also didn't want to add to the injury he obviously had over firing Shala. "I wish there was something I could do," I spoke up.

"You're doing it, you're with me and that's all a nigga need right now."

Fifteen minutes later, he pulled up to a big ass house and I had to do a double take to make sure I was seeing this house correctly. It was so big that you would think the governor stayed here or something. At first, I didn't think he was making that much money in his club but shit, seeing this house changed all that.

He had three other cars sitting in the driveway, a Camaro, a 2019 Audi and another Tahoe truck but it was white. He looked over at me with a goofy ass smile on his face, "What?" he asked.

"This house is huge. Why do you have the condo if you have this big ass house?"

"Because it's closer to the club, so if I need to get there I can. Now that you and I guess Kymani are staying there I'ma keep staying here."

Getting out of the car, he walked over to my side and grabbed my hand. He was making a habit out of holding my hand and I didn't know if I liked it or not. Usually I couldn't stand for a man to hold my hand especially not in public. I had a bad habit of not showing affection outside of the home because I wasn't affectionate with anyone in that way when I was younger or before now.

When we entered the home, I was in awe the chocolate painted walls blended so well the cream colored furniture and the brown and cream coffee table and end tables. "You can sit here, and I'll go fix us something to drink then we can figure out where we going for the weekend."

"Okay."

I watched as he exited the living room and went through some wood double doors that lead to the kitchen I guess and got up. I couldn't help myself, I had to look around to see if he had a woman staying with him or a family, I knew nothing about. A house this big he had to have some kids somewhere.

I walked all downstairs and when I made it back to the living room he was sitting on the couch with a blunt in his mouth, "Found what you was looking for?"

"I was just looking around, I wished I stayed in a house this big. I wouldn't know what to do with myself."

"If you stick around who knows you might be staying here."

Walking back over to the couch, I sat next to him and looked him in the eyes, "What are you looking for in a woman? I really don't think I can give you anything I mean I'm staying with you, working for you and I don't even have my high school diploma."

"We gon work on all that, I just want you to continue being yourself. You're real and that's something I'm not used to. A lot of people think of me as a maniac but I'm not I'm probably the coolest motherfucker that people will ever know but they can't see past the fact that I run a strip club and was in the streets."

"Well I think it's amazing that a man could even run a strip club and make sure that women are being respected even though you have your moments. Like today, why are you so quick to tell Winter and Barbie that their easily replaceable?"

"You don't know how long I've been putting up with them and they shit. Those two have really fucked up everything for me, I used to have more dancers than I do now, but they ran them all away."

"Damn, do you think they just think you're going to replace them because you don't like them? A few of the girls already feel like I'm the reason you're being extra hard on them like I'm making you change things. They don't like the fact that I don't have to take my clothes off for money and that you have me by your side all night."

"And that's all about to change. I don't want you stripping I told you that already. How do you feel about being a manger, but I can handle all the money shit?" he asked.

I didn't know what to say. The only thing I did know was I didn't want to be a manager and his crew still felt like they can disrespect me. I have a low tolerance for bullshit and as he seen I can handle myself if a bitch jump stupid but as a manager you can't be doing that. I don't want to be fighting stripper bitches all the time just because they feel like they're better than me.

"If you want this job for me then I'll take it but I'm not for all the extra bullshit that comes with being a manger."

"You don't have to worry about none of that."

We sat and stared at one another for a minute then he moved closer to me and kissed me on the lips. Leaning back, he climbed in between my legs and started roaming his big hands all over my body. When he got to my thighs he started to squeeze and rub closer to my pussy, "Mm," I let out while squirming underneath him.

He moved back and put the blunt back to his mouth, "You ain't ready for me," he chuckled.

"Boy please."

"Ima grown ass man," he stood up and grabbed his dick, "You not ready. I'll have your lil' ass going crazy."

I couldn't help but laugh, he was cute and cocky at the same time. That was the shit I liked most about him and the fact that he shows me that he actually care about me and not just trying to get in my panties was a plus.

After a while of debating, we decided to just stay at his house because I didn't want to leave Kymani out here alone knowing how crazy Mike's ass is. He respected it and we laid up for the rest of the night.

Kymani

This shit that was going on between me and Mike was really getting to me but not as much as it did when it first happened. I mean when you with a man that you know don't do nothing but sit in a trap all day and be around bitches and niggas all night it's liable that you gon' find yourself being a step mother to a child. Well, some of y'all, not I though.

I have had two miscarriages due to this nigga beating the baby out of me and I refuse to play step mother to a child that he didn't want to have with me, but he had with another bitch. He can figure that shit out for himself because Kymani was done, I was just looking for the right moment to reiterate the shit to his dumb ass.

He been blowing up my phone for the last day trying to see where I was, and I've been ignoring the fuck out of him. "Aye, my nigga been trying to get in touch with you. Why you haven't been answering his phone calls and shit?" Quez asked. I hated that I needed to come to the store because I knew I was liable to run into one of his homeboys' but Quez told every fucking thing.

"Because I'm not interested in playing step momma to a kid that he had on me. You can tell him that, because we both know you are."

"What the fuck that's supposed to mean?" he asked and another one of their other homeboys answered for me.

"Yo' ass be telling Mike everything. Like you can't have no secrets for yourself, that woman don't want to be bothered with that nigga, but you gon' go and let him know you seen her."

I laughed and shook my head, "Period!" Disappearing into the store, I grabbed me a big blue soda, some lays chips and went to the counter so that I could get me some cigars. I was hoping that Quez was gone by the time I made it out of the store because the last thing I wanted is for him to follow me to Dex's condo and Mike swear I'm fucking with that man.

After paying for everything, I grabbed the bag and rushed out of the store, "Fuck," I said to myself when I saw Mike sitting his car with that girl Jazz and their son. I didn't know why he was fucking with me when it was apparent that they were working things out for the sake of their son. "Kymani, bring yo' ass here!" He yelled standing next to his car.

"No, I have to be to work. Leave me alone please," I snapped never looking his way. Mike made me go weak whenever I looked at his mocha skin and coal black eyes. He was an evil nigga alright and my ass used to be following him around like a lost fucking puppy. I was so disgusted with myself after I left. Not believing that I was that weak behind a nothing ass nigga.

When I got to my car, I was about to open the door when he shut it almost slamming my finger in the door, "So, you gon' ignore me like I'm not talking to you?" he asked.

"Mike, I really don't want to have anything to do with you and I most certainly don't want to talk to you. Go get back in the car with your baby momma and son, leave me alone."

"The lady said she don't want to be bothered, so how about you leave her alone like she asked." A deep voice spoke behind us. Turning around, I was looking in the face of one of Dex's homeboy's named Dreux. I had always seen him around but never built up the courage to talk or speak to him no matter how many times he spoke to me, I never returned it.

"This don't have shit to do with you, how about you go mind your business somewhere else, because this is mine."

"No, I'm not. I'm done with you, I don't understand what part of that you don't get."

"None of that, before you found out about Jazz and my son everything was good between us and now you acting like something changed."

"Because it did, the fuck? You have a whole child with somebody you cheated on me with and not to mention you had her in my house. I could have been petty and beat her ass that day she showed up at my house, but it's not her fault that I was with a dog ass nigga."

"Kymani, go to the house so we can talk about this in private."

"You mean so you can beat my ass and lock me in the house for the next week or so. Nah, I'm good. You go on about your day sir," I told him before reopening my door and sitting down.

BAM!

He punched my window and all the glass fell on me making me shield my face, "Ah!" I screamed when a piece of glass cut me.

Looking up, Dreux had his ass by the collar and was dragging him back to his car. Quez and his other homeboy had their guns out but Dreux had the parking lot deep with his crew. My guess is they didn't fuck with one another and that's where most of this animosity was coming from. I didn't want to have anything to do with it, so I started my car and drove out of the parking lot.

I would get my window fixed when I got the money, but since my bitch was with her nigga for the weekend, I would just drive her car to work and shit. She wouldn't mind, but I was going to call to make sure. Pulling my car into the parking lot, I sat there for a while before calling Briana. The phone twice and she answered, "Hello?"

"Hey. I was wondering if I could use your car?"

"What's wrong with yours?" she asked, and I was going to lie and tell her that it stopped working but when she see it, she's going to know I lied so I told the truth.

"Mike saw me at the store and decided to bust my windows."

"Damn, that nigga trifling. Yea, of course you can use mine."

"Are you sure you don't mind?"

"Girl, it's fine. He can't do much to my broke down car," she laughed, and I joined in.

"I'll make sure he don't anyway. I just have to go to work tonight."

"It's fine Kymani," she urged like she was trying to rush me off the phone.

"Okay, bye."

Getting out of the car, I went into the building after looking around and making sure Mike wasn't stalking me. I still needed to go to the house to get my work clothes, but I also didn't want to run into him which I knew was slim to none. I'm pretty sure he probably got my apartment full of pills, weed, and crack but I had a plan for his ass.

I was about to terminate my leasing contract, so he was going to have to figure something out. As a matter fact, he better take that shit to Jazz's house.

As soon as I got into the condo, I took my shoes off and went to sit on the couch so that I could roll me a blunt. I wanted to clean up so that Dex wouldn't think I was just staying here. I didn't plan on being here long anyway, so I was about to find me a second job so I could move out and get me another place.

Once the blunt was rolled, I got up and put it to my mouth then lit it. Going into the kitchen, I put some music on and started to clean up.

Money by Cardi B came on and I couldn't help but rap along with her.

My bitches all bad, my niggas all real

I ride his dick in some big tall heels

Big fat cheeks, big large bills

Front, I'll flip like ten cartwheels

Cold ass bitch, I give Ross chills

After the kitchen was spotless, I took a break and relit the blunt. Sitting at the bar, I smoked half of it then went into the living room. I picked up everything and put them into the spare bedroom that I was sleeping in.

Grabbing the vacuum, I made sure everything was picked up off the floor before starting. Once that was finished, I went into the bedroom and put all my things back into my duffle bag, I decided to keep everything packed just in case, "There," I smiled when I looked around.

Everything was back the way I found it and now I was about to leave and attempt to get my work clothes from my house on top of talking to the manager. Walking out of the door, I got on the elevator and rode it down to the first floor.

When the doors opened, I saw that guy Dreux standing at the front desk. "Hey, I was looking for you," he said looking me up and down.

"For? And how did you know to look for me here?"

"Dex my homie, all I had to do was call and ask his girl if she had seen you and they told me to come here. You dropped this," he stated handing me my wallet that I hadn't even noticed was missing.

"Thank you, I didn't even know it was missing."

"No problem, can I ask you a question?"

"Sure."

"Why are you with that dude if he treats you the way he does?" His question caught me off guard.

"Um," I cleared my throat, "I'm not with him anymore. If that's all I have to go to my old apartment that he have taken over and get my things."

"What you mean taken over?"

"I mean he won't leave my apartment which is why I'm staying at Dex's place."

"So, I can make him leave."

"Nah, the last thing I need is a murder on my conscious," I let him know.

"It won't be my murder, I already don't like him."

"I have to go, thanks again," I said cutting that conversation short. I didn't know what Mike had going on in the streets and I didn't want to know. Whatever beef they have don't have anything to do with me and I wanted to keep it that way.

The sun was being so disrespectful today, that's how hot it was. Hotness and DopeBoys don't mix, that was a recipe for a murder. When I got to my car, I was about to unlock the door when he called out, "I'll give you a ride, so he won't fuck up your car up even more."

That was the whole point in me driving my car instead of Briana's, looking over my shoulder to him, he was standing next to a black Camaro with swanger's on the rims, "I don't want your car to get damaged all because you're with me."

"I'm not worried about that. If he even remotely fuck with my car, he gon' go into hiding so that I won't get at him." Dreux was fine and arrogant, that alone told me that's why he and Dex was such good friends. "It's just a ride, I'll keep my hands to myself and keep my cool unless he do some faulty shit," he added.

Deciding that it wouldn't be a bad idea to have him there with me. I reluctantly walked to his car, pulling the door opened, I got inside and sunk into the hot leather seats, "These seats will give somebody third degree burns on the ass."

"That's why you should have on some clothes to cover it," he chuckled.

When he got in the seat, he started the car and drove out of the parking lot. The entire ride, he kept looking at me with a smile on his face. He reached forward and turned the radio up, TI's song *Whatever You Like* was playing.

I didn't know what he thought he was doing or why I was smiling the way I was, but I liked it. "Watch the road and not me," I mentioned.

"Have you ever heard of multitasking? That's what I'm doing, I can't help but look at you, your beauty distracting me," he stated making me blush.

Finally, we got to the apartments, "Pull right here. I need to get out of my lease."

Doing as I said, he pulled into a parking spot that was close to the building and I opened my door, "I'll come with you," he offered.

"'You don't have to."

"But I want to," he pulled his door opened and got out. Walking around the car, I met him at the front and together we walked inside. "Can I help you?" Lela, the office manager asked looking at Dreux.

"I need to get out of my lease," I spoke up since she wasn't acknowledging me.

"Name?"

"Kymani Bridges."

She sat down at the desk and we sat in front of her. I watched as she typed some shit in on the computer then looked at me, "You just renewed your lease for six months. Why do you want to get out of it?"

"Because I'm not staying out here."

"You'll have to pay the rent for the next six months to get out of it."

When she said that, I put my head down and shook it, "I don't have that kind of money."

"How much is it?" Dreux asked.

"Her rent is seven hundred a month, so she'll have to pay four-thousand-two-hundred-dollars to get out of the lease."

"I'll pay it, cash or money order?" he asked.

I can't let you do that, that's a lot of money."

"Don't worry about it, I can pay it. That's nothing to a man getting money," he assured me.

"Money order," Lela told him.

"We'll be right back," he grabbed my hand and lead me out of the office and to his car.

"It'll take me months to pay you back," I didn't know what he thought was going to happened between us but I'm not for sell and neither is my pussy.

"Just go on a date with me and we'll call it even," he smirked.

"Um, I don't know. I'm not looking to date anybody right now."

"One date then we can see what happens."

"Fine, one date." Getting back into his car, he backed out of the parking lot and headed to the nearest store which was down the street. Pulling up, he cut the car off and got out. I didn't see no point in me getting out because I didn't have any money to put on this money order. I watched as he went inside then came out five minutes later.

"They had to put it on six different money orders but here it goes," he handed them to me.

"You really don't have to do this," I didn't want to sound unappreciative, but this was a lot of money for a stranger to be giving me.

"It's too late, if I didn't want to do it, I wouldn't have offered. Now, let's get the rest of your stuff."

"Thank you."

"No problem, I just don't want to see you with that nigga ever again. You deserve so much better than him."

I nodded my head, "Trust me, you won't have to worry about that. I'm done with him."

"Good." Driving back to the apartment, we pulled into the parking lot and got out. He grabbed my hand again and I pulled it back.

"Why do you keep grabbing my hand?"

"Because I don't want ole' girl in there to think she have a shot. She keep looking at me and it's creepy as fuck," he laughed.

"I know the feeling," I joked.

"Oh, you got jokes, huh?"

"Kind of," I laughed. When we stepped into the office, I sat down and filled out the money orders before handing them over to Lela.

"Okay, you're out of your lease."

"Can I get something that states that?" I asked. I didn't know her like that, she might be trying to fuck Dreux out of his money, so I had to make sure.

She hit something in the computer then went to the printer. When she handed me the price of paper, I read it through then shifted my name on the bottom next to hers. "That's it?" Dreux asked.

"Yep, thank you again. Now, I have to go get my stuff and hope I don't run into Mike."

"Let's go."

For the last time, I walked out of that office feeling good. I didn't have to worry about dealing with Mike anymore and it wouldn't be hard for me to find another place. We drove around the buildings until we reached mine, "Right here."

They had all kinds of people sitting on the porch and hanging out front. I was nervous as fuck when I got out of the car. It was like all eyes were on me and Dreux, "I got you," he reassured me as we walked passed the group that was sitting on the porch.

"Mike ya girl here," Quez spoke and Mike turned around then stood up when he saw Dreux behind me.

"I know you don't have this clown in my crib," he snapped.

"She do and what? She coming to get her shit."

"You do realize you're out numbered," Mike said chuckling.

"I'm never outnumbered, remember that."

They was sitting there having an ego and pride moment, so I slipped away and went into my bedroom. Grabbing my other two duffle bags, I stuffed the rest of my clothes and shoes in one then my hair accessories in the other one.

"So, you really leaving?" Mike asked standing in the doorway.

"Yeah, I told you I was done with you and I meant that. You might want to put this apartment in your name because it's not in mine no more."

"You know I love you Kymani. Don't do this to us."

Putting the last of my hair stuff in the bag. I grabbed them both and walked out of the room. "Sometimes Love isn't enough to make somebody put up with your shit."

Turning around, I handed Dreux my bags, we walked out of the house and got back into his car.

"You good?" he asked, I nodded my head and he drove off.

Mike

The fact that Kymani thought it was okay for her to bring that nigga here had me baffled. That was her second mistake, the first was leaving a nigga like me, she was never going to find another man that was going to put up with her like I did. Yea, I may have fucked up and got Jazz pregnant but if Kymani loved me, she would have tried to see past that.

"Are you okay?" Jazz asked walking into the house with my son in her arms.

"I'm good, I'ma have to find another place to sell out of because Kymani had her name taken off the lease and they won't let me put mine on there."

"I told you that she wasn't that dumb, I knew she wasn't about to let you keep her apartment and she wasn't staying here. You turned her place into a crack house, so it was no way she was about to let you ruin her name."

"You don't think I know that."

"Don't tell me you was going to try to work things out with her knowing that you want to work things out with me for the sake of our son."

"It's nothing like that. Kymani and I were together for a long time and it's hard to just let something like that slip through your fingers. I'm not saying I don't have love for you because I do, you have my first child and a son at that, but if it wasn't for him me and Kymani would still be together."

"So, you have love for me, and you love your son, but you blame him for you and Kymani not being together. I wish that you would open your eyes and see that you have somebody right here that's willing to be with you. No, you can't sell drugs out of my house, I have a child and the last thing I want him around is drugs all the time."

"I wouldn't put him in that position anyway. You don't have to worry about that, I'ma figure something out. I might buy one of these run-down houses and use that."

"Okay. Well, we gon' go I guess."

Getting up off the couch, I walked them back outside and to her 2019 black Malibu. Grabbing Luca from her, I placed him in his car seat and buckled him in before closing the door and going to her window. "I'll see you when I get to the house later," I said before kissing her on the lips.

I know I'ma fucked up nigga for being with two women at the same time, but now that me and Kymani was officially over, I could put that focus on my family. Jazz made it perfectly clear that I was either going to be a family man or I wasn't going to have one. She didn't want to be a baby momma and I couldn't say I really blamed her.

Standing back, I watched as she backed out of the driveway then went back into the house, grabbing the duffle bags that we had laying around. I stuffed the money and weed into one and the crack and pills into the other one. Even if they let me put my name on the lease, I wouldn't be able to keep the drugs here because that nigga Dreux seen where they were.

After everything was packed up, I walked out of the house and put them into my car then went back inside, "I want everything moved out of this apartment and put on the side of the road. If you find anything that you think might be important keep it so that I could give it to Kymani."

Just because me and her weren't together didn't mean I wanted her to miss anything that could possibly be important to her. She was a smart girl so I'm pretty sure she knew what she was doing when she got her name pulled off the lease. I put so much money into this place because I love her, and she said fuck me and the fact that we spent so much time and have so many memories in this bitch. She wanted me to pay for fucking up with her and that was the only reason she was fucking with that nigga Dreux. At least that was the only reason I could see her fucking with him.

Once everything was moved, I made them clean the apartment till it was spotless then we left. Getting into my car, I backed out of the driveway and headed to the front office so that I could give Lela my key. I also wanted to ask that bitch why she didn't let me know that Kymani was getting out of her lease, she could have stopped that shit if she wanted but she was another one that didn't want to see us together.

Pulling into a parking spot, I got out of the car and went inside, "Hey daddy," she smiled walking around the desk.

"Why you didn't warn me about Kymani getting out of her lease? You could have blocked that shit."

"I know I could have, but why would I help you keep her when she don't want to be kept? That nigga paid the remaining balance on her lease so I couldn't make her stay in it. She had her mind made up and a man that was willing to come off almost five-thousand-dollars to help her."

Something had to be going on between her and him for him to be willing to pay five grand for her to get out of a lease. Without another word, I handed her my key and headed for the door.

"Am I going to see you later on?" she asked.

"I doubt it, I got some stuff to handle."

"Do Jazz have anything to do with why you've been blowing me off?"

"'No, but if she did you would know that," I said before walking out of the office and getting into my car.

Driving off, I went back to the trap house that I had other workers in. The only reason I moved my drugs to Kymani's spot is because they had all the crack, weed, and pill heads out there. Pulling up, I cut the car off and got out, "What's up boss?" Cali, a dedicated loyal worker asked while sitting on the porch.

"Shit, how have shit been around here?"

"Business wise, not good. Half these niggas took the fact that you wasn't around to their heads and started tripping."

"What you mean?" I put a pre rolled blunt to my mouth and lit it.

"I mean them niggas was charging the wrong prices, putting what was for you up then pocketing the rest of the money. They have bitches in there smoking and fucking, just all kinds of shit. That's why I stay outside and out of the way."

"Aight, I'm about to put a stop to all this shit," I said blowing smoke out of my mouth and standing up. We both walked inside, and they sure enough had hella bitches smoking my shit out, "Anybody want to tell me what the fuck going on?"

I pulled my gun out and sat down.

"Who are you?" one of the females asked and I smiled.

"I run this shit, who the fuck are you?"

"No, I'm dating the man that run this shit," she snapped. Her confidence made me laugh until I seen the one and only Bang throwing out orders. When he seen me, he stopped talking.

"Nah boss, do your thing," I said leaning back in my chair. I loved when niggas who didn't know shit about running a drug operation tried to run some shit.

"It ain't what you think," he replied walking over and standing in front of me.

"You sure? Your girl said you run this shit, so I'm trying to make sure before I air this bitch out."

"I was just helping out around here. They was acting lost without you, so I picked up the torch."

"How can you pick up something that wasn't left behind? You letting niggas charge the clients more than what they supposed to pay and got these bitches in here enough for the cops to raid this hoe."

"Who you calling a bitch?" the same chick asked.

"Get your girl before I kill her."

"Naomi, shut the fuck up before he kill all of us," he told her, and she stood up.

"See nah, I see you ain't nothing but an errand boy, I'm good on you," she told him, and I fell out laughing. He learning at a very young age that bitches only fuck with niggas like us for the money.

"Damn, you gon' let your girl diss you in front of your crew like that?"

I was just fucking with him now, his ass better be lucky I didn't just come in here and start shooting. I wasn't about to let him get away with this shit though, "What you want me to do about it?" he asked.

"Nothing, however, I am demoting you to cleanup crew. Since you want to run some shit you can run that," I chuckled.

"Man, after all the work I put in for you. Cleaning crew?" he asked in disbelief.

"I didn't ask you to do nothing that wasn't in your job description, you wanted to play boss without asking."

"I was just helping, without you around this shit was going down the drain."

"I don't want to hear that shit, ayo Cali?" I called out and he walked back into the house.

"Sir?"

"I want you to take over for me. I'm going to be busy looking for a new trap house and since you're the only one that didn't follow this jackass' rules, I'm making you my new head nigga in charge."

"Got you, you won't have to worry about anything."

"Good, and if anybody have an issue with taking orders don't be shy about laying them down," I assured him and looked around the room at the many faces of people that have always worked for me. I dapped him up, "I'm counting on you to make sure shit stay good around here."

"You don't have to worry, I learned from the best," he smirked.

Nodding my head, I walked out of the house, got back into my car and backed out of the driveway, while driving through the hood I seen they had a house for sell a few blocks away and decided to take the number down.

It was getting late, so I decided to just take all my product and money with me to Jazz's place. She would never know I had it with me because I was going to put it in my other car that was sitting in the driveway so that I wouldn't have to hear her mouth. Her ass was always bitching about something, so I wanted to just minimize the arguments and spend time with her and our son for the first time in a long time.

*M*e and Dex were having such a good time together, I never knew that I could have so much fun with somebody and not be having sex. I mean it's not like either of us didn't want that, we both were just so hung up on getting to know one another that we didn't come around to it. We were now chilling with his sister's at his house and I was nervous because they both kept looking at me with mugs on their faces.

"So, what do you do for a living?" Dulce, the younger one asked.

"I work at the club your brother owns. I'm not a stripper though."

They both laughed, "Good, we all know he have a thing for strippers. You're not the first woman we've met that worked for him and he dated. Do you know Winter?" Rina asked.

"Yea, we got into a fight last week. She's such a bitch, no offense," I didn't know if they liked her or not, but I had to tell the truth about me not giving a fuck for her ass.

"Don't worry, we don't like her ass anyway. We both knew that she was only fucking with my brother for his money and although he didn't want to believe us in the end he found out."

"I think that's fucked up, I don't care what your brother have I like him for him and it's going to always stay that way."

"I like her," Dulce told him when he walked up with an older lady behind him. He had a frown on his face, and I had never seen him look so angry before.

"Who told y'all to invite her?"' he asked both Rina and Dulce.

"Nobody, we both just feel like it's time for you and momma to hash out y'all differences so that we could be a happy family like old times."

"I can't be happy with somebody that blames me for the death of our brother when it was his choice to go out there and be selling drugs not mine," he snapped.

Getting up from my chair, I looked at him, "Excuse me, I don't think this have anything to do with me," I said and tried to walk by him, but he grabbed my waist. "No, handle your business. I'll be in the house," I added.

"I don't want you to go anywhere. Stay here, one day you'll be family so you may as well know what you're getting yourself into ahead of time," he told me.

Nodding my head, I sat back in the chair and just looked at the woman. She didn't look old enough to have four children and I didn't know that his mother was still alive because he never talked about her and every time, I asked about her he would change the subject.

"I'm confused, y'all had an older brother?" I asked and everybody eyes shifted to me.

"Yea, but he died selling drugs and our mother blamed Dex for so long that he had started to believe that it was his fault, but it wasn't. How was he supposed to know that some niggas was going to rob Trayvion?"

I didn't know what to say, so I just closed my eyes and took a long breath. Now, I see why Dex was always so snappy at some people and why he didn't trust nobody with anything, because his own mother blamed him for his brother getting himself killed. I wanted to speak up on it so bad but knew that I couldn't. I most definitely didn't want to get into it with nobody over something I had nothing to do with.

"I'm sorry I blamed you Dex, I was going through a lot. Losing your brother and father weeks apart. I was just looking for somebody to take the hurt out on."

"And you took it out on me like I wasn't hurt as well. I'm the one that found him, you wasn't there you didn't see him until after the coroners and shit got there. I was the one that saw his face every day."

"Do y'all know who killed him?"

"No, whoever did it fell off the face of the earth. I looked day and night, high and low and could never find out who it was, and the streets wasn't talking. Nobody could tell me anything, no matter how many bodies I dropped looking for the killer. I couldn't find him."

I put my hand on his shoulder and laid my head on his arm, "It's okay baby."

"Nah, it's not. See you don't have siblings, so you don't know what it's like to lose one of them."

"I don't have blood siblings you're right but how do you think I felt when I had to leave the brothers that I had in my foster home?"

"I'm sorry, I didn't mean it like that babe."

"It's okay, I know how you meant it and even though they didn't die, they probably thought I was dead. Nobody knew where I was that's how good I was hiding, you can't find somebody that doesn't want to be found is what I'm saying."

"I know. Look ma I know what you was going through, that was my brother but that was your son and I don't have kids so I can't tell you how you should have handle that. At the same time you still had three other children to worry about and you said fuck us."

"You think I don't know all the wrong things I did? I will never forgive myself for the shit I put you and your sisters through, but they let me make it up to them and I'm hoping that one day you'll let me into your life as well," she told him. I don't know about him, but I believed everything she was saying to him.

He turned his head and looked at me, putting my hand on his forehead I wiped the sweat that had formed from the heat. "I don't want to deal with this right now. You're here already so I say let's make the best of the time we have together."

"I'm sorry, I didn't get a chance to introduce myself. I'm Gladys."

"Briana, nice to meet you," I smiled.

Dex stood and grabbed my hand. We walked towards the house.

"What you think?" he asked.

"About?"

"Should I forgive her?"

"Dex I don't know, I didn't have a mom, remember? But you can make the most of her being here now. You might not get this chance again."

"You right. Thanks baby," he kissed me on the lips. I watched as he went back over to his mother and sisters then went into the house. Seeing them all together had me thinking about the family I never had the chance to have. Heading up the stairs that was in the kitchen, I went into the bedroom and laid down.

Twenty minutes later, Dex was shaking my body and saying my name, "Bri, wake up."

"What's wrong?"

"Nothing, come downstairs and eat."

Sitting up in the bed, I stretched and yawned then climbed out of the bed. Sliding my feet into some slippers, I followed him out of the bedroom and downstairs. Everybody was sitting at the table with their plates already and he had me sitting next to his mother and him. I guess he didn't want to sit next to her but the way she was smiling told me that everything was going well.

"I'm glad you and my son have found each other, he deserve somebody that can see through his flaws and love him for him," she said throwing me off guard.

"Yea, I like Dex a lot, but we haven't been seeing each other that long for us to be in love."

"You say that, but I see the way y'all look at each other. That's love my child, I know that you're going to be my daughter in law I can feel it in my soul. You're the one for my son."

"Aight ma, stop before you scare her away." Dex chuckled and I joined in. She wasn't scaring me away, she just caught me off guard, but I guess it's true what they say; mother's know best. I had strong feelings for Dex, but I wasn't sure what kind of feelings those were just yet.

We were still taking things slower than a snail walking and that's the way I wanted to keep it for now. I felt like he is somebody that I could see myself with in the long run, but I didn't want to give him too much props or put him on that pedestal that other women put their men on. Men like him don't stay faithful for too long, they start looking for things that they aren't getting at home from somebody else and the last thing I want is for this man to hurt me because I was blinded by the love I may have for him.

I've seen it so many times, and with everything that I endured as a teenager I don't want to go through that again. I've been in relationships with grown men at the age of fifteen, when I didn't have anywhere to go, I was sleeping from pillow to post at a different man house every other week and I had to come off my pussy for that.

I've had men tell me that they wanted to see me win and those same men were the ones making sure I didn't come up. They knew if I came up, I wouldn't need them so they did everything they could to make sure I needed them. I didn't catch on to that until I got older then I started learning for myself that men some hoes when it comes to a woman getting her own.

"Don't mind her." Dex whispered in my ear.

"Oh, it's fine. I'm not tripping on that, if anything I'm honored that she thinks I'm the one for you. That's something I never heard before."

"So, tell us about your life? Who are your parents?" Dulce asked.

"Um, I don't know who my parents are. I was placed in a foster home at the age of eleven and I was molested by the husband, so I ran away. I had to make sure I could take care of myself and that meant me doing somethings I didn't want to do."

"Like stripping?" Gladys asked.

"I'm not a stripper, but I have slept with men for money and a place to stay."

"At the age of eleven?"

"No, I didn't run away until I was fifteen."

"I didn't know you went through any of that," Dex spoke putting his hand on mine.

"You never asked about my past. It's not a secret. I've been through somethings and I had to figure out a lot of stuff by myself at an early age."

"You ever got pregnant?" Rina asked and Dex shot her a look that told her to shut the fuck up.

"No, it's fine. I did, I got pregnant when I was sixteen, but the man beat the child out of me when his wife found out."

Yea, I been through some shit and nobody would have ever guessed it unless I told them. I never really talked about that with anybody because I didn't want anybody to judge me for even getting pregnant, but they didn't understand the shit I went through at that age. I went through stuff that no child should ever go through, not to mention I never told anybody about me being molested. I know that people will think I'm crazy for trusting Dex as much as I did, but he proved to me that he was a good dude. He never tried anything with me that I didn't want, that alone made me trust and have respect for him.

"Did you ever tell on the husband?"

"No, it would have been his word against mine and he had me thinking that what we were doing was okay until I got older. He used to sneak into the bedroom when I was sleeping since I had my own room and undress me. His wife used to be working double shifts at the hospital."

"Who is he?" Dex grimaced. I could tell by the look on his face that he was fucked up about hearing this shit. That's why I didn't want to tell him, on top of him never asking. I was fine with that, but now that his mother and sisters' were sitting up here asking me all these questions it made all the memories come back full speed.

I was able to forget some of things without thinking about them, but now I couldn't help but think about how fucked up it was that happened to me.

"Briana, what's his name? I know you may not remember but I need you to think. I want to have a conversation with him and see if he remembers this shit."

"Dex just leave it alone," I urged.

"Nah, he got away with molesting you. His wife never questioned why you ran away? Nobody ever looked for you. They probably just thought you was trouble and didn't want to be with that family without even looking into the father."

"I'm not the only one that he did it too, it's a few other girls but we're all too old now to do anything about it and killing him won't do anything for me. I'll still see his face when I close my eyes."

"Briana, what if I don't kill him? What if we just go talk to him?"

He was pressuring me into doing something I didn't want to do, and I was so close to giving in until his mother spoke up, "Dex you can't make her want to see that man, just leave it alone. Don't pressure her into doing something she don't want to do."

"Okay," he sat back in his chair then got up, "I don't even want to eat anymore," he added and walked away from the table.

"Excuse me," I told them before getting up and following him downstairs into his man cave. He was now sitting in front of the flat screen with a blunt in his mouth. "I know this is all new to you, but I don't want you to get locked up by going after this man. He's going to get what he deserved, I just want you to promise me that you won't get involved."

He cocked his head to the side and shook his head, "How can you even ask me to sit up here and promise you that? I care about you, that's why I want to make this nigga pay. Please let me avenge you. You deserve justice."

"Killing him is not justice, that just means you'll go to jail for doing it. He's not worth it, I'm telling you," I was pleading with him, shit begging him. I didn't want to see Dex in jail for doing something that's not going to solve anything. I hated Dade with everything in me, but he lost everything. His family, his wife hell I heard that his own sons' don't fuck with him.

"You right about that, but it might make you feel better."

I was starting to see what everybody was saying about Dex, his ass was ruthless and reckless. He didn't care what anybody had to say if he wanted to see somebody dead, he was going to make sure it happened. He didn't care about the consequences like the way I cared about him, "If I knew you was going to want to do all this, I wouldn't have said anything about it. Maybe it was my fault because I could have said something, but I chose not too because I thought that were my family."

"That shit is not your fault, I don't ever want to hear yourself blame you for that fuck shit that nigga did. This is exactly why he need to be taken care of. He don't deserve to be here on this earth, he damn sure don't deserve to be breathing the same air as you baby."

"Dex, let it go," I urged, and he chuckled then put the blunt to his mouth.

This wasn't a disagreement we were having, I wanted to know that I could tell him something and he wouldn't result to killing everybody. You can't go around killing everybody that did you something when you was a kid, I had numerous of times to say something, but I didn't.

Dade had me believing that he loved me, but I found out later on in life that he was using my young body to get his nuts off. I didn't know any better and I blamed my parents for that, if they wouldn't have put me up for adoption then I wouldn't have been in that predicament in the first place.

"Briana, I care about you. I'm going to say this once and only once, I want to get at that nigga for you. I don't care about you being mad at me, but I can't let this shit go. If you was my daughter, I would have been killed his ass, all I have to do is make one phone call."

"But I'm not your daughter, I'm your girl. I can handle my own and I think I have the right to say if I want somebody murdered or not. I don't want you to kill him, he's not worth it and I don't want his murder on my conscious."

He sighed then stood up, "I'll be back," he said and walked out of the man cave. I sat on the couch and heard the front door slam, not being able to stop the tears that was raining down on my face. I laid on the couch and got it all out before getting up and going back upstairs.

"Well, I don't know where he went but if y'all ready to go then it was nice to meet y'all," I told each of them.

"Yea, I have to get home." Gladys spoke hugging me, "You're strong and he may be pissed off, but he'll come to his senses."

I hoped that she was right, I watched as they all walked out of the house then went into the kitchen. After cleaning it up, I went upstairs, took a quick shower then got in the bed.

I was pissed off at the fact that Briana wouldn't give me the name of the nigga that molested her. I didn't give a fuck how long ago it was, I meant it when I said he didn't deserve to be still living and walking around free when he was the reason that she lost her innocence at an early age. She didn't understand that she had a nigga that could make one phone call and get anybody murked. I may not be in the drug business any more but that didn't mean I didn't have the contacts that I did before.

Everybody knew who the fuck Dex motherfucking Luthor was. I made moves, I was the reason that a lot of niggas was eating in these streets. I put a lot of these niggas on and they didn't forget. I was driving down my old block that I used to sell on and I saw my old homeboy Pat chilling at the park.

Raising down the window I stuck my head out, "Ayo Pat, stay right there!" I yelled then busted a U-turn in the middle of the street and headed over to where he was.

They had some females out there with them and they was looking trying to see who I was, "What's up my nigga?" he dapped me up when I got out of the car and walked over to him.

"What's good? You still have Trav number, I need to holla at that nigga about something," I said without going into details.

He nodded his head then pulled out his phone and scrolled through his contacts. Handing me his phone, I put the number in my phone then gave it back to him, "What you up to tonight?" he asked.

"Shit, about to make this phone call then head back home to my old lady. I see you still out here doing your thing."

"Yea, you know them crackers can't keep me down for long. They thought that lil' time they gave me was going to teach me a lesson, but you can't teach a nigga who always had to get on his own. I didn't have nobody breaking their backs to make sure I had it, you know we miss you on these streets."

"I bet, but the streets can't get anything out of me. I gave them all I had and when the time came, they wasn't trying to look out for a nigga."

"I feel you on that, let me introduce you to some ladies. I know you say you have an old lady at home but that didn't stop you when we were younger."

"Key word my nigga, younger. I'm too old to be playing them girls, plus I got me a winner and I'm not trying to fuck that shit up for nothing or nobody."

"It won't hurt to get introduced." Pat was the reason why I lost my first love and the child that she was carrying for me. When she found out that I had cheated on her with one of Pat hoes, she aborted my child and took off without letting me know. I didn't even know she was pregnant until I ran into her mother a while back.

"Ladies, this my nigga Dex. You may have seen him around or at his strip club called Baby Dolls. Dex, this is Lani, Kiara, and Khelani."

"Nice to meet all of y'all," I smiled at each of them. They wasn't bad looking either. Lani had to be the baddest of them all because she was light skinned, she didn't have a scar in sight and her lips were juicy and pink. The other two were bad built and you could tell they had hella kids just by the stretch marks that was on their stomachs and shit.

"You're cute." Lani flirted. "Where you been hiding him at?" she asked Pat.

"I haven't been hiding him anywhere. He don't fuck around with the fuck around and don't let them pink lips fool you Dex she's crazier than a Betsy fucking bug. You don't know how many females I had to stop from beating her ass because she was stalking their man and them.

"Damn."

"If I like what I see, then nothing is going to stop me from getting it," she licked her lips.

"Well, don't like me. I have a girl and I'm not looking for anybody else to do anything with. It's nice meeting you though," I told her before dapping Pat up and heading back to my car. When I got in, she walked over to me and handed me a white paper with her number on it. "What this for?"

"Just in case you change your mind. I don't bite unless you want me to."

Shaking my head, I held the piece of paper up and nodded my head. Driving off, I put the number in my cup holder and headed back to the house, on the way there I grabbed my phone and called Travis.

"Who this?" he answered.

"Dex, my nigga what's good?"

"Dex Luthor, damn nigga last time I talked to you, you said you was done fucking around."

"I know, but I need you to look into somebody for me."

"Anything specific?"

"A foster family, her name Briana."

"Briana Kane?" he asked.

"Yea, how you know her?"

"I saw her a few days ago, she didn't tell you she know me. We grew up in the same hood together before she ran away. I don't even need to look into her background, her foster family name is Barbra and Dade."

"What happened to the Dade character?"

"I don't know, last I heard he moved to a secluded area because they had people out to kill him for something that he did."

"Molesting kids. He did it to Briana and that's why I'm trying to get at him."

"Do she know this? I'ma tell you what I know bro, but he had Briana thinking he was in love with her and that's why she didn't say anything."

"Nah, she don't, and I want to keep it that way. If you can look into this Dade nigga and try to give me some locations to look, I'll appreciate it," I said then hung up the phone. Putting the phone back into my cup holder, I pulled up to the house and Briana was standing outside with Dreux and Kymani.

Getting out of the car, I walked over to her and grabbed her arm, "Why you grabbing me like that?' she asked looking down at her arm.

Letting her go, I just looked down at her, "We need to talk." Walking into the house, I waited for her to walk in behind me and when she did. She sat on the couch next to me and just looked at me, "Why didn't you tell me that you was in love with this nigga Dade?"

"How do you know his name? And because I thought I was in love with him, I didn't know what we were doing was wrong."

"But it didn't stop you from letting him do it to you."

"If you really think I let him slide his dick in me every night then you're just as ignorant as him. I don't have to deal with this, I'm out," she snapped.

Not saying anything, I watched as she walked out of the house and then threw one of the glass vases that was sitting on my coffee table at the door. I didn't know what the fuck was coming over me, but I was pissed the fuck off that she didn't keep it all the way real with me. She could have told me, and I wouldn't have judged her at all. I know how easy it is for you to think that you have something with somebody older and then that shit get switched up and turned it into something total different.

That nigga knew what the fuck he was doing, I don't think I'm that mad at her I'm pissed at the fact that she didn't say anything to anybody, but I guess people handle shit like that differently.

"What happened?" Dreux asked walking into the house.

"I found some shit out about her and I'm pissed that she didn't say anything about it."

"You mean when she was younger? You can't be mad at her for not saying anything when she was younger, be happy that she feels a strong enough connection with you to tell you about it. She could have let that shit stay inside and not say anything to you or anybody."

"I know that, I'm happy that I know but now she don't want me to get at that nigga."

"And I'm guessing you ain't gon' listen and now y'all at odds."

"What you trying to say?"

"I'm saying that it's easier for a girl like her to be looking for love in the wrong places. She probably didn't think what they were doing was wrong because she fell in love with him and the whole time, he was using that as his advantage. He knew that she wouldn't tell what he was doing to her because she loved him."

I thought about what he was saying, and he was right, but I wasn't about to tell her that. Sooner or later, she was going to come to her senses but either way I was going to handle this shit and I'll deal with her being mad at a later date.

"You right, but I'ma still get at this nigga."

"And you know I'm with you till the wheels fall off, but I want you to be ready for the backlash that you probably gon' get from her for doing that."

"I'm ready for it already, one day she gon' realize that I'm doing this for her. I don't want that nigga walking the same earth as her, he deserve to be in hell for what he did to her."

"This shit is really eating you up, did something happen to you when you was younger my nigga?" he asked me, and I just looked at him.

"Nah, nothing like that. When Dulce was five, she got molested by our father's brother and that shit haunted her for a long ass time until I killed him. Nobody wanted to believe that he did it, not even my father he swore up and down that our uncle wouldn't do no shit like that."

"Did he ever admit it?"

"He didn't have to, I knew it because of the way he always looked at her and how scared she used to be when he was around."

"That's fucked up, but why don't you just tell Briana that and maybe she would understand why you're going so hard."

"I don't know, now she's mad at me and probably won't talk to me because of how I went about that shit." Leaning forward, I grabbed a blunt that was sitting on the table, put it to my mouth and lit it.

Taking a long drag from it, I let the smoke sit for a while before blowing it out. "I know you might don't want to hear this right now, but I know Briana and Kymani going out tonight if you want to go."

"I don't know, I'll think about it," I told him.

"Alright, well I'ma get out of here. Hit me up later if you decide to come through bro." We dapped one another up and he walked out of the house.

Later on, that night, I called Briana's phone and she didn't answer. I was getting mad frustrated because I had been blowing her up since she left, and her ass wasn't answering. I didn't think she was that fucking mad that she would start ignoring a nigga.

Getting up, I went into the restroom and took a quick shower. When I got out, I dressed in some black Levi jeans, a dark blue and black Versace shirt and on my feet were some Versace loafers. Looking in the mirror, I brushed my hair to make sure my waves were on point then walked out of the room and downstairs.

Grabbing my keys to my black Camaro, I stepped out of the house and got right into my car. Starting it up, I sped out of the driveway and headed to Club Ego. A brand new club that's only been opened for a few weeks, pulling into the parking lot. I parked right next to what I knew to be Dreux's car and got out.

With each step I took, all eyes were on me. The women were yelling trying to get my attention and the men looked at me with envy in their eyes, "What's good Dex?" the bouncer spoke when I walked up.

"What's up?"

We dapped one another up and he gave me a brotherly hug before letting me into the club. Stalking through the club, I saw Briana and Kymani on the dance floor dancing like they didn't have a care in the world. When she looked up our eyes met and she smiled, throwing her a nod I went into the VIP section where I saw Dreux and sat down.

"Why you didn't hit me and tell me you was coming?" he asked.

"Because I'm grown, what's been up? This hoe packed as fuck."

"I'm saying, I'm surprised you got in, they been talking about locking the door for the last hour, so I didn't think you was coming."

"I had to think about it for a second, but you know can't nobody keep me locked out of a club."

"Hell nah, not when you can stop their business. This nigga been telling the crowd that he hoped you stopped by so that you could see how he was doing."

"Yea, he doing good. You know niggas look for our approval in this shit."

"Facts. Your girl been bugging though, she been dancing on niggas and they been buying her drinks all night."

"Oh yea?" I chuckled. I was trying to hide how pissed off she was making me, but I wasn't going to say anything. When I snapped, she was going to see the side of me that nobody liked. She was going to know and understand that I didn't tolerate disrespect of any kind.

I watched as Dreux poured me a drink and downed it then poured myself another one. I saw a dude walk up behind Briana and instead of her pushing him back, she started to twerk her ass on him while his hands roamed all over her body. Sitting the cup down, I got up, "Bro, what you doing?" Dreux asked.

"I'm about to see something."

Walking out of the section, I went down to the dance floor and stood right behind her. She was backing her ass up until it was on my dick, then she turned around, "What are you doing?" she asked.

"Why you dancing on all these niggas like you ain't got one?"

"Because I don't. My nigga wouldn't be asking me no fuck ass questions about some shit that happened years ago."

"I asked you that because that's what I heard."

"And my nigga wouldn't be checking up on my story like I have something to lie about. You so used to fucking with bitches that need you to save them that you don't know how to act when somebody telling you to just let shit go."

She tried to walk away from me, and I grabbed her by her arm, "Don't walk away from me when I'm talking to you Briana."

"Let me the fuck go Dex, look I don't have time for this shit. I came out to have a good time not argue with you so if that's all you looking to do then you can leave me alone."

Her mouth was really getting to me, I wasn't used to a female talking to me the way she was. A part of me wanted to knock her the fuck out but the other part of me wanted to kiss her, "When you fucking with a nigga like me, you should be used to me getting in your business especially when it's something as crucial as that shit."

"Why are you so invested in killing Dade?"

"Why aren't you?"

"If you insinuating that I still love him then no, I don't. If you want to kill him then be my guest, but it won't make me feel better actually it'll make me feel worse. I don't need you to do that, what I need is for you to be here for me," she told me.

Nodding my head, "You coming home with me?"

"I don't know, I'll think about it. You showed your ass, so I don't know."

"I didn't show nothing, now if you want me to show my ass, I can show you how single Dex get down ma."

"Show me," she smirked then licked her lips.

Walking off, I went back up to the section and sat down. They had some women come in there and one of them sat dead in my lap. I was about to push her ass off when I spotted Briana looking with a frown on her face. If she wanted me to show her how single Dex got down, then she was about to be mad as fuck for the rest of the night.

*I*t's been about a month since I last heard from or seen Mike and I must say it was marvelous not to have to worry about getting my ass beat whenever something didn't go right for that man. Dreux has been trying to get me to go on another date with him since our first one and I've been dodging his ass as well, he had too much shit going on for me to really fuck with him like I wanted to.

Thanks to him, I got my own place and a brand new car. He helped me out so much that I was able to get a new job and go back to school for my degree in business management. Something I never thought I would do.

Briana was sitting on my brand new all white sectional rolling a blunt when I walked into the living room, "So, what are you going to do about Dex?" I asked plopping down next to her.

"What you mean?"

"Girl... everybody can see that you're not happy being his arm Candy whenever he have a function."

"I mean I'm happy, I just want to be more than his arm candy. Everything between us is good sex wise but the communication is off, and I barely see him."

"Do you think he's back in the streets?"

"I don't want to believe that but all the out of town trips he's been taking and staying out all night is telling me otherwise. I don't know, I want to talk to him, but I'm scared of how he might react."

"We both know that man will never put his hands on you. He loves you even if neither of y'all had said it yet."

"I don't know. He's changing and not for the better I'm afraid," she frowned and put the blunt to her mouth. I watched as she lit it and took a long drag from it, it was like she had something on her chest that she wasn't ready to face.

"What's wrong Pooh?"

"I think he's cheating on me."

"Nah. Dex wouldn't do that to you."

"He wouldn't? I mean if he's in the streets then somebody got to have his attention which would explain all the late nights and trips if it ain't drugs."

She may have had a point, but he could be doing anything, I mean Dex isn't a man that likes to stay in one place for long and she told me herself that he has invited her on these trips and each time she declined.

"Talk to your man, get an understanding and tell him you're not going to sit back and let him cheat on you with the streets or any woman."

"And then what? He be mad at me and don't speak to me for days? What would that prove?"

I shrugged; I didn't know what she wanted me to say. It wasn't my relationship and she didn't want to take my advice so she would have to figure this one out on her own.

"Enough about me and Dex. What's going on with you and Dreux?"

"Nothing. He's been blowing me up for some time and I keep ignoring him. I just don't think I'm ready to get into another relationship with a drug dealer."

"I understand that but he's not Mike. He actually cares about you so you should at least talk to him," she stated.

"Hmm, I'll think about it."

We sat and smoked for a lil' while longer until her phone started to ring. She didn't budge to grab it, so I did and handed it to her. The look she gave me told me that she didn't want to talk to Dex, but she didn't have a choice, his crazy ass wasn't about to come around here acting a plum fucking donkey.

"Hello?" She got up from the couch and went out on my balcony. I had a nice two bedroom condo out in Oak Cliff. I had a job that was close to my home that I only worked part time and the rest of my time I spent doing homework and shit. I haven't been out since the last time we did go out.

Ten minutes later, she came back into the house and sat down, "What happened?"

"We have to catch a flight to New York tonight."

"Ooh for what?" I smiled.

"I have no clue and I really don't want to go. He didn't call to see if I wanted to go, he told me I had no choice as if I'm his slave and have to do what he says."

"And that's what I don't miss about being in a relationship. Look just go and if you don't want to be there let him know. You can't be unhappy and going on trips even if it is to New York."

She cocked her head to the side but didn't say anything because she knew I was right. She loved that man with everything inside of her even if they hadn't been talking for long, she loved his savage ways.

"I have to go," she sighed and got up. I walked her to the door and let her out before shutting and locking it. Going to sit back down on the couch, I grabbed my phone and looked at Dreux's messages before texting him back finally.

Me: What are you doing tonight?

I waited a few minutes to see if he responded and like clockwork he did.

Dreux: Something with you, I hope.

I guess it was safe to say I had this man hooked on me and I haven't even given up the goods. He was so sweet to me but ruthless in the streets. Women couldn't stand to look at me knowing I had a man like him wanting me and nothing to do with them.

Raising up off the couch, I grabbed my purse and keys so that I could go to the mall just in case Dreux wanted to take me out. He said he wanted to do something but not what, so I wanted to be ready because he's a spur of the moment type of dude.

Walking out of the door, I got into my car and made sure my air was blasting because on a day like this it's suicide to be riding around in a car with no air. That's how hot it was. The ride to the mall was smooth, my phone kept going off and I knew that couldn't have been Dreux because he rarely called.

Stopping at the red light, I pulled my phone out of my purse to look at it when I saw that it was Mike blowing me up. I didn't know what the fuck he wanted and I damn sure wasn't about to call him back, I should have gotten a new number when I got this new phone.

Sitting the phone in between my legs, I continued the drive then switched lanes when the Galleria came into sight on my right hand side. Pulling into the parking lot, I found a front parking spot by luck and got out of the car. Looking into the mirror, I fixed my hair and lip gloss before going inside.

It was so packed that some of the stores had lines all out of the doors. I was about to ask if they had a sell going on when I realized that it was Friday. Everybody and they momma was getting their outfits for the club tonight, "I'm so happy I don't be on the club scene like that anymore," I said to no one in particular.

"Girl me too. They acting like the shit gon' go out of style or something." A girl standing next to me spoke and we shared a laugh. The line for the store we were both waiting in line to go in started to go down. When we stepped inside, she picked up a dress and showed it to me, "What you think?" she asked.

"You could pull it off," I smiled. She was gorgeous, her long honey blond hair had me looking at mine like I needed to get something done to it and that would be my next stop after I left here. She was light skinned and had the prettiest hazel eyes.

"I'm Miracle, but everybody calls me Winter."

"Kymani, everybody calls me Kymani," I laughed.

"It's nice to meet you Kymani."

We walked around the store and found what we were both looking for, the dress I picked up was black, but the back was out which was good because this weather was ridiculous. "Hot date tonight?" I asked when I saw her picking up a pink dress that was similar to mine.

"Something like that, I'm trying to get over my ex."

"I know the feeling, niggas be forgetting that we were the ones that held them down and put our sexy on hold for them to feel secure only for them to move on with the next bitch."

"You ain't lying about that. I was with this guy for about eight months but now he got this new girl and have her thinking that me and his relationship wasn't that serious. I don't understand what they get out of lying to the girl."

"That's fucked up. My ex had a whole baby on me and still had the nerve to think that I was going to stay around. He used to put his hands on me all the time and my dumb ass stayed with him, I let him do me dirty a hundred ways before leaving him and now I'm sort of seeing somebody new and he's nothing like my ex."

"I think you win the having the worst nigga. I hope that you and your new boo work out."

Getting in the line, we kept talking until it was my turn to check out. Putting my things on the counter, I watched as the girl rung up all my things then looked up at me, "The total is two-hundred-seventy-dollars and twenty-two cent," she said.

Handing her three hundred dollars, she handed me my change and I turned around to leave the store, "It was nice meeting you," I told the girl and she handed me her phone.

"Give me your number, maybe we can go out to dinner or to the club one night."

"I'm down with that," I said entering my number into her phone and giving it back to her.

Walking out of the store, I went into the store over and grabbed me some black and gold strapped heels. After I paid for them, I left the store and mall. The walk back to my car, I thought I had seen Xila and a few of her other friends. Stopping, I paid close attention to the girl and realized that it was her and walked over to them, "Hey Xila," I spoke, and she just looked at me.

"Kymani, what's up girl? You look so different, you have a glow to you," she hugged me.

"I guess that's what happens when you leave that toxic nigga alone," I joked, and we shared a laugh.

"We have to catch up, I don't want to hold you. Is your number still the same?" she asked.

"Yea hit me up girl," I said before hugging her again and heading to my car. Getting in, I threw my bags in the backseat and drove off. On the way to the hair and nail salon, my phone started to ring yet again and this time it was Dreux, "Hello?" I answered.

"What we doing tonight?" His deep voice asked.

"I don't know, you tell me."

"I was thinking dinner and then we can come back to my place and watch movies and chill."

"I'm down with it."

"You just want to be around a nigga, admit it. You miss me just as much as I miss you."

Not texting him may have been killing me, but I wasn't about to admit that shit. "Not really, I knew I was on your mind because you stayed texting me. I had to make you wonder about me before chilling with you again."

"Well, you accomplished that baby girl."

"Okay, well I'm about to get my hair and nails done so I'll talk to you later," I told him and hung up the phone.

The drive to the nail and hair salon wasn't long and it was a good thing that they were attached. When I arrived, I got out of the car and went inside, it wasn't packed thank God. "Nails or hair?" A black chick with some long ass braids asked.

"Both."

"Follow me," she turned around and I followed her to the back, "This is Kym, she's going to be doing your hair and nails today. If you have any questions don't hesitate to ask," she added before leaving me.

"Have a seat, we gon' start with your hair. What do you want me to do to it today?" Kym asked twirling me around in the seat and lifting it up.

She ran her fingers through my hair, and I was confused as to what I wanted until I saw a picture of a girl with a short bob, "I was thinking about cutting it into a short bob and dying it black or auburn."

"You sure you want to cut it? It's so long and pretty."

"Yea, I need a new look, I want to look like a new woman when I get out of this chair," I let her know.

"Okay, well let's get started, shall we?" She took my hair out of the ponytail, leaned my head all the way back and started to wash it. Once she was finished washing and conditioning it, she wrapped a towel around it and sat me up. Next, she dried my hair then started cutting all my dead ends off, the short cut was nice, and I was loving it already. After, she finished cutting it, she started to dye it the color I wanted and rewash it, "Ooh, I like this," she smiled as she blow dried my hair.

My hair was now in a fro, I watched as she parted and started to flat iron in sections until she was finished with my whole head. My hair may be short now, but it was still thick and because of who my parents are, my hair would be growing back in no time and hopefully more healthier than it was before. "I love this color on me," I boasted swinging my hair from side to side.

"Me too, it looks so good on you and trust me not everybody can pull off this color, but it suits you and your brown eyes perfectly."

"Thank you."

She sprayed some holding stuff on it then brushed the falling hair off my shirt and took the apron off of me as well, "Go sit in that chair and I'll come do your nails as soon as I finish cleaning up."

Doing as she said, I went to the chair that was five inches in front of me then sat down. Looking through the colors, I found the one that I wanted which was a dark green color. Sitting it down, I watched as she swept the floor and cleaned off her hair supplies before coming over to me, "I want this color."

"You must have a date tonight?"

"Something like that," I blushed.

Just thinking about seeing Dreux had me blushing and smiling like a school girl, I just hope he's able to keep this smile on my face all night long. "Well, I hope he's ready for you because you a bad bitch," she laughed, and I joined in.

"I hope so as well, I just don't want to be too sexy if you know what I mean."

"You don't want him to think that he's about to get any of your goods."

"No, I like him, but we haven't been knowing each other that long and I just got out of a bad relationship, so the last thing I need is for a man to be pressuring me into sex."

"Lay the rules down when you get with him, let him know he don't run shit and for him not to expect shit from you. Especially not on your first date, you're a beautiful woman so I'm sure he's going to try to butter you up, but you already know you're fine so that'll just be him boosting your confidence even more."

That was one thing we could agree on, I've always known I was a bad bitch and even if I may not be the baddest bitch in the world. I knew a lot of bitches wasn't fucking with me when it came to looks and loyalty.

It took her about an hour to finish my nails and toes, but I wasn't complaining. When I got out of the chair, I paid her then grabbed my keys and headed for the door when I saw Jazz sitting down getting her nails done as well. She turned and smiled at me while I walked out and to my car, "Aye Kymani, come here!" Mike's voice invaded my mind and I shook my head with disgust.

"I'm good, and I have somewhere to be."

"I'm not playing with you girl, come the fuck here. I'm tired of you ignoring me like I don't exist to you anymore."

"You don't Mike, you have a whole family and I want nothing to do with you, now if you don't mind. I have to go."

"So, you seeing that nigga that saved you at the store that day huh? You know I find out everything."

"Mike, I don't give a fuck about you finding out squat. I'm grown and gon' do what I want to do as long as I'm single. Bye," I arrogantly told him while getting into my car and leaving.

I couldn't believe Kymani was acting like she didn't fuck with me before. I mean I understand I fucked up and I'm still fucking up by being with Jazz, but if she wasn't going to be with me after finding out about them then fuck her bald-headed ass.

Jazz and I were out at a restaurant on a date for the first time in a long time, I hadn't took her out since she had my son and that shit went down with Kymani. I don't know at first, I thought that she showed up at Kymani house just so that we would break up but then I slowly started to realize that she really wanted to be with me. We were talking when I looked up and saw Kymani walking inside with that nigga Dreux.

I watched as they got seated and everything, "Are you going to stare at her all night?" Jazz asked.

"Nah, I'm sorry I just don't want to be in the same vicinity as her and ol' boy," I honestly told her.

"Mike, if you want to make things work with us then you're going to have to be okay with being around Kymani without feeling no type of way. You can't expect her to sit in her house and mope about you and you're not going to make me stay in the house like you used to. I told you I'm tired of being a secret and it's time for everybody to see that I'm here to stay."

Looking at her, I could see the way I was acting made her feel some type of way and that was the last thing I wanted to do. I love Kymani, I do but I can't keep treating Jazz like she doesn't matter to me. She's the mother of my child, so I at least owed it to her to make things right especially since I lied to her when we first got together.

"I should have told you about her," I let out.

"It's fine, I mean I wanted to hate you for it, but it wouldn't change the fact that you're the father of my child and we're going to have to be in each other's lives no matter what, but I do want to make something clear."

"The floor is yours, I will now listen to how you feel and do much better than I've been doing."

"Okay, that's good to hear. I want to make it clear that if we do this, you will not treat me like you treated Kymani. It's a lot I'm not going to take and if you can't get with the program then you gon' be alone at the end of the day."

"What you mean? I gave her anything she wanted."

"So, she wanted those black eyes and busted lips? Yea, it didn't take long before people started telling me about how you beat and cheated on that girl every chance you got. I'm not her, I will never be her and I want you to understand that. I'ma grown woman with a child so if you can't treat me right then we don't need to be trying to figure anything out."

She was right, I did Kymani dirty when we was together, and I regretted that shit every day I woke up. Maybe, if I had been good to her, I wouldn't have to worry about making things work with somebody else. This was all my fault and I knew I had to do better if I wanted to be happy in my life. The last thing I wanted was to be like my father, he used to do the same thing to my mother and now he's in jail and alone.

"You don't have to worry about me treating you like I did her. I know I did some fucked-up things to her, but that makes me want to be a better man."

"Good, do you think you'll start to hate me and Luca for ruining what you had with her?"

Grabbing her hand, I looked into her big brown eyes and smiled, "I could never hate you or my son. I know I haven't been the best man to anybody, and I don't even deserve this chance being with you, but I'm grateful that you want to see the best in a nigga. My son makes me want to be a better man not just for you but for him as well, I don't ever want him to have to wonder what kind of man I was because I fuck up what we have. He deserve to have both of his parents' in his life."

"You're right about that," she smiled and let my hand go.

We finished eating our food, I threw four hundred dollars on the table which was more than enough to cover the cost of our bill and give the waitress a hefty tip. Jazz walked ahead of me and I was close behind her, as we passed up Kymani's table, I could feel her burning a hole into the side of my face.

Turning around, I looked at her, she looked happy and the last thing I wanted to do was ruin that for her. Grabbing Jazz's hand, we stepped out of the restaurant and it was raining hard as fuck, "Stand here, I'ma go get the car."

"Are you sure? I don't mind getting wet with you."

"The only thing I want you getting wet for me is the bed sheets," I chuckled before running to my 2019 black Charger. Hopping inside, I started it up and drove to the front of the restaurant. When Jazz got into the car, I looked back into the restaurant and Kymani was still looking at us.

"It's so cold," she shriveled. Leaning forward, I turned the heater on for her so that she could get warm. I didn't want her to get sick but shit she was soak and wet.

On the way to the house, my phone was ringing back to back and it was Lela. She didn't know how to take no for an answer, and she was pissing me the fuck off. I was trying to do better for Jazz and Lela was trying to fuck that shit up.

"Mike, answer your phone. It may be important."

"Trust me, it's not plus I just want to spend some quality time with you while Luca is with your mom."

"It feels like I haven't had a night out since he's been born."

'That's because you haven't, you been making sure he was good."

Jazz has always been with Luca, day in and day out so tonight I wanted to make sure she knew how much I appreciated her for never bitching or nagging about me coming home late or being gone all day.

"On the real, I couldn't have asked for my child to have a better mom."

"Thank you, I love my lil' man," she smiled.

When we pulled into the driveway of our five bedroom, six bathroom home, I spotted Dreezy sitting in his car with the door cracked and smoke was coming out of it. "What the fuck this nigga doing here?" I asked parking my car next to his and getting out. I handed Jazz my keys so that she could get into the house and went over to his car, "What you doing here?" I asked pulling his door opened.

"Man, we need to talk."

"What's up, make it quick. It's cold then a motherfucker out here."

"That's that Texas weather for you, aight remember how easy it was for us to take over the streets with Dex out of the way."

"Yea?"

"Well, I just got a call that he's taking over the Mexican cartel. You know the one his father built, he's about to come for us I can feel it."

"Yo, you serious? I don't want to go into a frenzy over a rumor."

"I would never lie to you about no shit like this and my people always tell me facts. They would never lie to me."

"Aight, well we can discuss this some more tomorrow. A nigga need to get out of these clothes and chill with my lady for the rest of the night before crybaby Luca come back."

He laughed, "Yea, I know moms probably pulling her hair out with his ass," he said, and I couldn't help but laugh myself. Luca was so spoiled behind his mother that it was ridiculous. We dapped one another up then I headed into the house, walking inside Jazz was standing there with a towel in her hand.

"You cold huh?"

"Hell yea. It's cold then a motherfucker out there."

Grabbing the towel from her, I went upstairs and straight into the bathroom. Turning the hot water on, I stripped out of my clothes and stepped inside. Standing under the water, I had to add some cold water because that hot water was burning my ass cheeks.

Closing my eyes, I shook my head I couldn't believe that they letting this nigga take over a big cartel like the Mexican's. He's going to have everybody in his back pocket and that was the last thing I needed. Dreezy was right we all know we gon' be the first people that he fucked with, so it was important that I either got in good with him or killed his ass. The choice was his at this point.

One thing I know is Dex is not fucking with me when it comes to these streets. He wasn't even that big when he was out here, he just got street creed because he was quick to off a nigga over any little thing. After showering, I got out of the shower and wrapped a towel around my waist. Walking out of the bathroom, Jazz was laid in the bed in nothing but her bra and panties, "You getting in the bed like that?" she asked.

My dick had a mind of his own and he was hard as hell, I been wanting to get back inside of Jazz, but she made it clear that we wasn't fucking unless I gave her the commitment that she wanted from me and she got it. She was the only female I was trying to fuck with deep.

"I guess, if you gon' give me some. I'm not about to get in the bed and get up with blue balls because you want to teach me a lesson."

"I'm not trying to teach you a lesson, I just wanted you to know that you can't expect to get pussy every night. Some nights I be exhausted, and I know y'all men don't think staying home and being a mom is a job, but it is."

"I get it, I do. I have to take that into consideration, I know it ain't easy."

"Good, that's about to make my next question easier. What you think about my mother moving in with us so that she can help me with Luca?"

"I don't know, if that's what you want then I'm not tripping."

"You sure about that? I don't want you to be uncomfortable."

"Your mother don't make me uncomfortable, it's just she be trying to pressure me into asking you to marry me and I don't want to deal with that."

"She what?"

"I know she just wants what's best for you and Luca, but I don't think we're ready for marriage but that's something for me to think about. I don't have an issue with her moving in here."

"Okay," she said and laid down.

Nodding my head, I grabbed my weed tray and walked out of the room so that I could go into my man cave and smoke. She didn't like when I had the whole house smelling like weed, so she made me move my smoking down there, it felt like my house wasn't my house anymore and I was fine with that.

"*A*re you having fun?" Dex asked walking into the bedroom of our Villa that he rented in New York. No, I'm not having fun, your ass is barely here. That's what I wanted to say but I didn't, because I didn't feel like arguing with him.

"I wish that you were here more than at just night time."

"I know, I'm sorry but I been handling business. I know you're not used to me having to work all the time but that's what happens when I come out of town. I be working."

"Okay." Getting out of the bed, I went out on the balcony and sat down in one of the chairs. Our villa was overlooking some buildings, but it was peaceful down here. He was so sure that we were going to spend time together but every time we make plans to do something he has to cancel at the last minute. At this point, I was just ready to go home and let him do his own thing out here.

"Do you want to go home?" he asked walking out and joining me.

"I mean I thought this was a vacation so that me and you could spend more time together, but it seems like I'm the furthest thing from your mind and if that's the case then I may as well go."

"Briana it's not like that I swear, I will try to do better. I didn't think I was going to be this busy coming out here, I was only supposed to come out here for a meeting, but they want me to take over the business."

"And what business is that?"

I already knew what it was, but I wanted to hear it from the horse's mouth. If he was going to get back in the streets, I didn't want to be anywhere near them, I've heard the stories about him when he was in the streets back in the day, but I never paid them much attention because I didn't know who he was but now that I do, I'm scared for myself and everybody else.

"You really want to know?"

"Yea."

He looked me in my eyes then grabbed my hand, "A drug organization. It was started by my father and a whole bunch of Mexicans and he want me to take over for him."

"I thought your father left you and your sisters' when you was young?"

"He did, but we recently found each other and that's who I've been spending all this time with. We've been getting to know one another and now he wants me to be the heir to his throne."

"Wouldn't you have to move out here?"

He put his head down and I let his hand go, standing up I shook my head and went back into the house. Walking out of the bedroom, I went downstairs and into the kitchen. I needed me a strong drink so that I could calm my nerves, if he thought I was about to move my whole life out here just so that he could run some drug organization he had another thing coming for him.

"What is your problem now? It seems like all you want to do is argue and I don't want to do that, I want you to move out here with me."

"It don't have nothing to do with you moving out here, I'm not moving my whole life out here. I like you a lot Dex, but I can't see myself moving out of Texas right now."

"Why? What's holding yo in Dallas, Texas besides a job that you work at my club? You could come out here and find yourself."

"That's not the problem, I don't have an issue with finding another job. I told you I only worked at the club to get fast money, that I needed but moving to a different state is different. Why do I have to uproot my life for you?"

"I'm not making you do anything that you don't want to do, but I'm really thinking about taking him up on his offer and I would like for you to be with me. I don't want to live life without you."

"Dex..." I stared but he put his finger on my lip to shut me up.

"You don't understand, I love you ma. You're the one I want to spend the rest of my life with, that's just what it is. Even if you don't love me, I love you and I'm willing to do whatever I have to, so that you could see that."

"You love me, but you're asking me to leave my friends behind so that you could run some streets. You can do that back home? Why New York?"

"Business, I can open up more clubs and you can run all of those. I don't want you to give me an answer right now but in the next month or so I will need one if you still want to be with me then I want you here with me."

I didn't say anything because it wasn't nothing for me to say, he had already made up his mind and it was no talking him out of it but if I didn't come then that mean we wouldn't be together anymore. I knew he wouldn't be faithful to me if I was in another state away from him but moving is too much work.

He leaned in and kissed me on the lips, sweeping me off my feet he carried me back upstairs and laid me on the king sized bed that was sitting in the middle of our bedroom. "We'll stay in this house, I brought it before we even came out here. I want you to be my wife someday," he said while planting kissed all over my cheeks, lips and neck.

Moving down, he slipped my panties off from under my dress and threw them on the floor. He picked my legs up and put them over his shoulders, this was his favorite thing to do when he couldn't have his way not that I'm complaining, "Mm," I moaned out while arching my back.

Looking down, I watched as his tongue flicked back and forwards on my clit. He then inserted two of his fingers inside of me and started to push them deep into my pussy, "Ahh, oh shit!" I yelled out in pleasure as he moved them in and out of me.

He raised up and kissed me on the lips still sliding his fingers inside of me. He sped up and the sound of my juices splashing all over his fingers and hands made him go back down to my lady pond. Removing his fingers, he replaced them with his mouth and cleaned me up. I watched as he sucked on my clit a lil' while longer before coming back up, "Can I slide inside of you?" he asked, and I nodded my head.

Without a word, he got out of the bed and removed his shirt, pants and boxers. Climbing back on the bed, he put my legs back on his shoulders and was about to put the head of his in when I stopped him by putting my hand on his chest, "Condom?"

Sighing, he got out of the bed and went over to the dresser that was on the other side of the room. I watched as he pulled it out of the pack and slid it on his ten inch curve dick then walked back over to me.

When he got in the bed, he laid down and motioned for me to climb on top of him. Planting my feet flat on the bed, I raised up while grabbing his dick and sliding down on it, "Ooh," I let out. I had to take a moment to adjust myself to his size before starting.

I don't care how much we fucked, I could never get used to his size. It was almost like he grew bigger every time we fucked. "Ride daddy dick," he encouraged while I slowly bounced up and down.

Putting his arms around my waist, he pulled me closer to him then put his mouth on one of my breasts. He sucked, licked and softly bit down on it all while aggressively bouncing me up and down, "Oh shit. I can't take it!"

"But you taking this big dick. Stop running from me," he growled in my ear.

I started to twerk and bounce on his dick and we kissed each other so passionately that I was sure everybody felt it. Slowing down, I started to grind my pussy on his dick then move in circular motion, as much as it was hurting, I wasn't trying to make him cum quick.

Flipping me over, he rammed his dick deep inside of me and laid there. "Kiss me," he demanded, and I turned my head towards him and took his tongue into my mouth. As I sucked on it, he pumped in and out of me very slowly, I'm guessing he wasn't trying to cum quick either.

"Hmm," I purred throwing my head back.

Raising up, he put my legs over his forearm and bounced inside of me as hard as he could then pulled out. Sliding back inside, I wrapped my arms around his neck so that he wouldn't keep doing that because I was scared that he might make the mistake and slide in my asshole and that was something I wasn't ready for.

"What's my name?" he asked pounding me.

"Dex!" I screamed.

"Wrong answer, what's my name?" he asked yet again.

"Daddy! It's daddy!"

"Mm, you got my dick so fucking hard," he groaned in my ear before pushing himself deeper inside of me. He started to drill me with no warning and my pussy was farting and I was so embarrassed.

Putting my hand on his chest, I was trying to push him out of me, but he knocked my hands off and pinned them down on the bed. Raising my body up some more, he pumped and pounded me like he was trying to punish my pussy for doing him something, "I'm about to cum!"

"Cum all over daddy dick. I'm not finished with you," he told me before pulling out. He stroked his dick a few times then pulled the condom off, "Suck it."

I looked at him then sat up, grabbing his dick by the base I stroked it up and down before sliding him in the back of my throat. I wanted this shit to be over with, his dick always had my jaws hurting because it was so big. I sucked and licked my tongue all over his dick while playing with his balls.

"Aw shit," he grimaced with the ugliest face.

I knew he was on the verge of cumming, so I pushed his dick further down my throat and started to tighten my muscles so that he wouldn't be able to move it.

He grabbed a fist full of my hair and started to fuck my face with no mercy, pushing his dick all the way down my throat I gagged until his nut flowed freely down it. "Fuck!"

When he was finished, I laid back in the bed and he collapsed next to me. Pulling me closer to him, he grabbed my face and turned it in his direction then kissed me on the lips, "I love you Briana."

"I know you do."

"I hope you think about making this move with me. I want to be with you for the rest of my life."

"I know and I'm going to think about it," I let him know.

Rolling over on my stomach, I put my arm across his stomach and went to sleep.

* * *

The next morning, I woke up and he wasn't lying next to me, "Of course," I said to no one in particular. Getting out of the bed, I went into the bathroom to handle my personal hygiene.

"Baby!" Dex yelled walking into the bedroom.

Pulling the door open half way, I peeked my head out at him, "What are you yelling for?" I asked.

"I was just making sure you was in here, where you going today?"

"Home, I hope. We've been gone long enough, it's time to go back home."

"Ah, I can't leave. Business, but I can get you home on the private jet if you want me to."

When he said that, I just shook my head and looked at him. I knew this was going to happen that's why his ass fucked me the way he did he wanted me to not be mad about him staying here today, but he thought wrong. I was pissed the fuck off and wanted to cuss him out but that would have to wait.

I had a lot of shit to do when I made it back home, especially since he gave me the role as the boss filling in his position while he was gone. I wanted to get out there and have a meeting with the entire staff including Winter and Barbie. I had to let everybody know that things were about to change around there, I'm not Dex and I'm not going to let anybody get away with disrespecting me or my role.

"I can't believe you're staying knowing that we had to have a meeting with the entire crew tomorrow."

"Babe, I know and I'm sorry."

He sat on the edge of the bed and I walked over to him, standing in front of him he put his hand on my shirt and pulled me down to him. "There isn't a way that you can leave and come back the day after."

"I don't know, I'll see but I know they need me here for something I just don't know what yet."

Sitting down next to him, I could see that me leaving and him staying was getting to him but unlike him I had to go back. I couldn't just up and leave without letting my friends know and if he had the same type of love, I had for my friends then he would go and let Dreux know.

He turned his head to face me then leaned in and kissed me on the lips, "I'll be safe, but I'm ready to go home."

"I know you are, it's a good thing I already called and got you set up to leave in the next two hours."

"For real?" I was trying to hold my happiness back. Not wanting him to think I was happy about leaving him, but I was happy about getting back home so that I could turn up with my bitch for her birthday.

"Yes, for real so get your stuff together and I'll take you to the airport."

Getting up, I started to get dressed. Sliding a pair of black ripped jeans on and a white jersey cropped top. Putting my Nike slippers on, I turned his way, "I'm ready."

"You sure about that?" he asked looking at my feet.

"Yea, do you have an issue with my slippers. I want to be comfortable."

"I guess," he shook his head and laughed. He got up and wrapped his arms around me, pulling me closer to him and kissed my lips again, "I'ma miss you but I'm going to try to make it back to you before the week is out. I don't want to be away from you for too long because niggas gon be trying to fuck with you."

"You don't have to worry about that, and you know that, you're the only man that I want."

"Better be. Aight come on."

He grabbed my bags and we walked out of the bedroom and down the stairs. Stepping out of the house, we got into the 2019 Tahoe that he rented, and he took me to the airport. Holding my hand, the entire way, when we got there, I just looked at him. Not knowing what to say, I leaned over the console and kissed him on the lips, "I'm going to miss you."

"Same. Hit me when you land."

"I got you." Upon getting out of the trunk. He hugged me so tight that I could barely breathe, he was acting like he wasn't going to see me again and that kind of had me scared. I also knew that Dex could handle his own in these streets just in case anything ever went down. I had faith that he would always make his way back to me.

He walked me to the private Jet, and I climbed on without looking back. If I turned around, it would only make me leaving that much harder.

I was really hoping that he came with me, but I guess other things are important to him other than me. Again, I couldn't be mad because I knew who he was when I got with him, but I didn't know he was going to get back in the streets.

Sitting in my seat, the flight attendant walked up to me and handed me a blunt, "Oh, thanks," I smiled up at her then put it to my mouth. She lit it for me then walked away. I guess this was courtesy of Dex so that I wouldn't be nervous. My phone started to vibrate, so I took it out of my pocket and looked at the message from Dex.

Dex: I miss you already. I can't wait to get back to Texas.

Me, I just couldn't wait to land back home. I was about to show my ass for my best bitch birthday and she better be ready too.

I was relieved when Briana left, I loved being around her and having her around that it made me not want to do what I was doing out here. I didn't want to take over for my father but being his only living son, I didn't have a choice plus I needed his connections if I wanted to get at Dade. I let Briana think I was leaving it alone, but the truth was I been having Travis look into that shit, but he couldn't find anything on him. It was like he vanished off the face of the earth, but he can't hide forever.

"You ready for today? I need you to have your game face, I need you to go in there and show them workers why I chose you to take my spot."

"I need to know why you chose me to take over for you as well. We haven't talked since before Trayvion got popped and now suddenly you want me to be the head of a cartel that I don't know shit about."

"I know you may think this is shady, but I promise you that I will never put you in a fucked up position. We haven't had no feds sniffing around since I took over. I had to make sure everything was put into a safe and businesses were opened so that we could clean all the money. I believe in you and I want to keep this cartel in the family."

"Luis, this shit is not easy for me. You're asking me to leave my whole life behind to take over for you when your team don't even know me. The only thing that they know is you don't trust none of them to take over."

"That's not it, I trust my people just not enough to take over and make sure shit stay the same. Believe it or not, I trust that you're going to make sure everything stay the same, people been waiting on me to step down for a long time because they didn't like how I was running shit."

"And you think I'm going to do your dirty work for you?" I haven't been in the streets in a long time and I don't think this is right for me."

"If you want answers about Dade then you need to want to take this. I can't make you do anything you don't wanna do, I can handle my own dirty work that's not the problem. The issue is I'm getting too old for this and I have enough money saved up to sit on my ass and just watch the rest stack."

"Aight." The only reason I'm doing this is because I need to get at this nigga. If it wasn't for him then I wouldn't be in this shit at all, he would have had to hand this shit down to his day one or somebody he didn't know. I hated being in the streets even when I was slanging, I'm risking my life for motherfuckers who wouldn't do it for me.

"You good? Let me know if you can't handle this and I'll put somebody else in that spot."

"Nah, I got it. You just better hope your people ready for me, if I feel like I can't trust them they some goners. I'm not risking my freedom for people I can't trust and if I have to kill everybody and start over then that's what I'll do. Let me be clear, I don't answer to no one so let your other people know that when I want to talk, they'll know."

"I have somebody you need to meet before you can fully takeover."

"Who is that?"

The front door opened and in walked one of the most notorious drug dealers from Mexico named Roc Gonzales. "I'm Roc and this is my daughter Isabelle. Let's get down to business."

"Uh, I'm not understanding what the lady have to do with anything that's going on."

"You want to tell him princess."

"It states that I must marry the heir to Luis's throne, and he can have the entire organization at his fingertips. It looks like you're that heir, so we have to get married."

"Ah, I don't know about that. I have a girl back home and I can't explain this shit to her or be with her if I get married to somebody I barely know," I looked around the room to see how serious they was and the looks I got back told me they were pretty serious.

Isabelle wasn't an ugly chick, she just wasn't my type. Not like Briana, she was full blown Mexican and skinny as hell. "I know this all seems sudden, but my father has been preparing me all my life to marry Luis's son," she said as if that was supposed to make me feel any better.

"It's business, you get married and stay married for 2 years and you won't have to answer to me or Luis because the organization will be yours."

"I have to think about this, you asking me to marry a bitch, excuse my French that I don't know all so that you could keep this shit in the family!" My voice roared.

Shaking my head, I walked to the door, looking back at Luis I nodded my head. He was lucky I didn't kill his ass for leaving my mother and his children when we needed him the most, he had nerve to show up at my brother funeral like I wasn't going to know that was him. I may not have seen him much, but I would always know my father.

"Remember, hustling is in your blood son. Make them feel you!" he yelled as I walked out of the house and shut the door behind me.

My phone started to ring as soon as I made it to my car and it was Briana, I'm guessing she finally landed and was calling to let me know. I missed her so fucking much that I had wanted to hop on the next flight and go home but I was going to do this and make sure everything was straight before heading home.

"What's up?" I answered.

"Hey, I just landed. I miss you."

"I miss you too, I have to handle some business, but I'll be home if not this week then next."

"Okay, just don't get into too much trouble out there."

"I won't. I'm making sure we're set for the rest of our lives."

"You're so hung up on me being your wife ain't you?" She laughed.

"'I am, and I know you feel it as well, you know we're meant to be together."

"We'll see about that. I'ma let you go," she said, and we hung up the phone. I didn't know what was holding her back from telling me she loved me, it wasn't like she didn't feel that way about me. She knew she loved me just as much as I loved her, the difference is I didn't have to hide my feelings for her.

She may have been fucked over by a few niggas, and I hated to be one of them, but she was going to have to understand that I did this for her. All the moves I'm making is for me, her, and the future.

Making my way to the warehouse, I pulled into the parking lot and parked my car right in front of the building before jumping out. Smoothing my clothes out, I walked into the building and they had a mixture of women and men in that bitch, "Hey, you must be the boy that's taking over for Luis." One of the women spoke.

"I am but I'm far from a boy. Don't refer to me as a boy ever again, I'ma grown ass man. I'm the boss and I want to get something clear with all of y'all. I know half of y'all been working with Luis for a long time, so this is exclusively for y'all. If you have an issue with me, come to me and we can handle it like grownups. I don't do well with motherfuckers trying to fuck over me or fucking with my freedom. I don't play that all talking shit, just like Luis will body anybody for disloyalty I will do the same."

"So, what? We're supposed to just believe you know how to run a drug organization. What do we know about you? Nothing. Luis and Roc both out of their rabbit ass minds."

"If you want to know what Luis was thinking then you can take that up with him, but if you would never question him, don't question me. I single-handedly took over my streets in Texas and I plan on making sure that this organization stay on the streets."

"What you gon' do about the niggas that's been coming for us?"

"I haven't heard about none of that but enlighten me."

"Okay, they have this young nigga named Clarence that's been gunning for us ever since he stepped on the scene out here. We don't know who the fuck it is, we never even seen him before."

"You mean to tell me that Luis never thought to look into this shit? He tripping, if he comes across me then I'm going to shoot his ass the fuck up. One thing I do is look out for my people, I don't need nobody to do my dirty work for me that's something I've never been scared of."

"Do you still run shit down there in Texas?"

"Nah, believe it or not, I was able to retire from the game two years ago. I moved into a mansion and opened some strip clubs so that's the only reason I'll be going home."

"Do you have a wife?" Another female asked sitting next to me.

"She's not my wife yet, but she will be. I'm not looking for nobody to fuck with while I'm out here. She may be in Texas but she's here in my heart so keep your legs closed to me ladies, I'm taken," I smirked at her.

"Well, excuse me for admiring how sexy you are. I'm Melina."

"Nice to meet you."

She sat next to me and started to rub on my leg, moving it away from her, she laughed, "I always get what I want."

"Not with me you're not. I advise you to stay away from me if you love your life."

"Oh, you serious about her. Your father was the same way about his wife until one night he fucked me right here on this table."

"And that's one more reason I need you to stay away from me. I would never fuck somebody that fucked my father. I don't know what kind of shit you're used to but I'm the boss around this bitch now and shit is about to change."

She sat back in her chair and looked around at everybody, "Get back to work," she told them.

"I got this, I don't need nobody to speak for me. I want to have a one on one with each of y'all to see what y'all about and make sure I can trust you."

"One thing you don't have to worry about is not trusting anybody in here, we're a family and we make sure we take care of each other. I want you to remember that, your father may have been our boss, but I run shit in this warehouse." Melina smirked at me.

She was testing my gangsta and didn't know that she was about to get murked if she didn't stop, "Not anymore, I run this shit and if you have an issue with it take it up with Luis. Ain't no woman going to be running shit this way or stepping on my toes, so take heed to this, if I ever catch you trying to run shit around here I'ma make sure you get a front seat when you're in heaven."

"What are you trying to prove? We have a system around here, I'm just doing what Luis told me to."

"I don't give a fuck what Luis told you to do. You gon' do what I tell you to do, now go back to your work station and stay there."

I could already see that I was going to have an issue with a few of these workers, so I was about to bring my nigga Dreux into the fold and some of his niggas. At least I know I wouldn't have to worry about them folding on me or snitching. These niggas wasn't about shit and these bitches wasn't doing shit except fucking and sucking dick.

I'm about to bring this shit back to the old days when females only worked in the warehouse and not outside. I didn't need any of them thinking they were running shit in this bitch. Getting up from the chair, I pulled my phone out of my pocket and walked into the office that was on the other side of the building, "What's good my nigga?" Dreux answered on the second ring.

"Ayo, how fast can you get to New York?"

"How fast you need me there?" he asked.

"Tomorrow and bring some of your most trusted workers. We're about to show these New Yorkers how we run shit in Texas," I chuckled.

"No doubt."

We hung up the phone and I sat down at the office. Looking through a lot of the business stuff I seen that my father had a club, a country club and a few clothes and shoe stores up around New York. He was really out here doing his thing and now his son was about to reign over all this shit.

I just hope they ready for a nigga.

Briana

When I made it back to my new apartment, the only thing I wanted to do was sleep in my bed. Yep, you heard right, I moved out of Dex's condo two weeks ago and I've been loving having my own spot. I didn't have to worry about him coming over and running shit and I most certainly didn't have to see his ass every time he pissed me off which was a plus. I don't know why I wasn't ready to use the words I love you, but I just couldn't say them. It's like every time I think I want to say them they get stuck on the back of my throat.

I guess I still am, and will always be, that girl who has to protect herself from being hurt even if that meant holding back my true feelings. Every time I think I'm feeling somebody something happens and make me feel like I'm not worthy of love.

When I was young all I wanted was love, I fell for man after man until I just couldn't do it anymore. It's like my heart turned cold because the motherfuckers I was willing to go against the grain for wouldn't do the same for me.

I was tired of feeling like I'm the one who is always giving her all and the man I'm with don't. Look at Dex, after telling me that he was happy that he was able to retire from the streets he decides it's a good idea to just hop right back in. He didn't do no digging to see why his father just suddenly left him the organization and that was fishy as hell.

One thing I did know, was if his ass got locked up; I wasn't waiting on him because I told him I didn't want him to do this in the first place but of course, a man gon be a man. I, however had my suspicions over it but it's nothing that I can do. I don't know anybody in the drug business especially not something like that.

There was a rapid knock on my front door, and I got out of the bed. Slowly walking to the door, I looked through the peephole and saw Kymani, Winter, and Barbie. "What the fuck is she doing with them?" I asked myself before pulling the door open.

When my eyes met with Winter, she rolled them and I did the same, "Wait you two know one another?" Kymani asked as they stepped into my home.

"These are the two girls that jumped me."

"Hold on, what?" She looked at Winter who shook her head.

"It was a misunderstanding."

"And now I'm your boss. As of today, I'm the new boss of Baby Doll's."

"Congrats bitchhhh, why you ain't call and tell me?"

"I wanted to wait until I got back, I have to have a mandatory meeting with the girls so they could know I'm nothing like the old manager and I'm not about to be running around for them like I'm their assistant," I said looking at both Winter and Barbie.

I hoped hem bitches knew they were on thin ice with me. I'm not Dex and as soon as either of them think they gon' cross a line with me they'll be getting escorted the fuck out of my club. "I can't believe Dex handed the club over to you. Do you even know how to run a club?" Winter asked.

"Dex taught me everything I need to know."

"I don't think sucking dick qualifies you as a boss," she smartly remarked and her and Barbie started laughing.

"Chill out, it's my day and the last thing I need is y'all to be arguing. Briana I'm sorry I didn't know these were the two you have issues with. I think they're cool but if you don't want them there tonight, I'll understand."

"No, it's your day and I'm not going to ruin it for anybody not even these two bitches."

"Good, so what's first on the agenda?"

"I don't know about y'all, but I was just about to take a nap. That flight kicked my ass."

"Is Dex back as well?" she asked sitting on the couch.

"No, he stayed back in New York to handle some unfinished business. We had a good time though."

"Good, I was worried about you after our last talk."

"It was nothing, I was having my own issues you know how that gets for me. I like him I really do, but I'm scared to trust him with my heart I don't want him to break it."

"Look, I know we never seen eye to eye, but you should be careful with your heart. Dex will have you thinking you're the only woman for him then boom another female takes your place." Winter chimed in.

"I don't think that was the case for you and him. He said that you two weren't serious for you to be fighting me and what not."

"If he thinks that then he's crazy, honey I was pregnant for him that's how serious we were and when I had the miscarriage, he was there all the way. Never left my side."

"I didn't know about any of that."

"Why would you? You only been knowing him a few months."

She was right, I hated to admit that, but Winter is right. I don't know enough about Dex to be in love with him no matter what my heart feels. If he hid this from me, I wonder what else he's hiding from me. Getting up, I went into the kitchen and grabbed my weed tray and cigars that was sitting on the counter.

I didn't feel like going anywhere this early, so the least we could do is smoke, and I needed this blunt after that shit Winter just laid on me.

The way I was starting to feel was like he kept that shit from me for a reason which is fucked up either way, it took a while, but he knows everything I've done and everything that's been done to me and he knows I hate not knowing the whole story to a relationship.

"No wonder you were so gonehoe on getting at me. I'm sorry I didn't know, and I feel bad."

"On the real you can't blame yourself. I knew what me and Dex had was over even if he still made his way to my house after it was over. When he started seeing you, he stopped all communication with me which told me that he really liked you."

"You think so? I don't know sometimes I feel like he's only with me because he took pity on me when we first got together. I know y'all probably felt like oh she's pretty there's no way she went through anything, but I did. I was homeless staying with my friend and the day I got the job at Baby doll's I didn't see myself catching feelings for him, but it happened, and I wouldn't take it back for nothing."

"I feel you on that, the only thing I can tell you is to be careful like I said before. Don't think that you're the only one getting attention from Dex, he's a hoe to the max and he thinks he's so smart that the women will never find out, but we always find out."

I heard what she was saying and the only thing I thought was if he was indeed cheating on me it would be hell to pay. I'm nothing like the women he was used to fucking with. "Briana, let me talk to you in the kitchen." Kymani spoke standing up.

Getting up, I handed the blunt to Barbie and followed her into the kitchen, "What's up?"

"Look, I'm happy that you and Winter made up, but don't trust and believe everything that's she saying. She may have known Dex longer than you have, but how do you know she's not just telling you this so that you would blow up at him?"

"I don't know which is why I'm not going to say anything to him until I know for sure that he's fucking up. I know not to listen to everything Winter is saying."

"Good."

We walked out of the kitchen and went back into the living room, but Winter and barbie were gone, "Hmm, where did they go?" I asked looking around my place. There was no sign of them and that made me suspicious of them.

"They on some other shit and I don't have time for it. We can go out and do something for my day but them hoes cannot join," Kymani snapped.

"Maybe she had an emergency."

"Or maybe she was just here to gather information about you and Dex so that she could run and tell whoever. I knew I shouldn't have trusted her and now I feel stupid."

"Don't feel stupid yet, I'm pretty sure they're going to be there tonight, and we'll get the answers we need until then it's your birthday and we're going to have us a good ass time," I smiled at her.

"Call me tonight when you get up. I'm about to go home and take me a nap so that I could be ready."

"Facts, me too," I giggled and walked her to the door. When she walked out, I shut the door behind her and locked it. Going back into the room, I laid back on my bed and called Dex, the phone rang twice before going to voicemail then it vibrated letting me know I had a text.

Pulling the phone away from my ear, I looked at it and saw that it was Dex.

Dex: Hey baby, I'm busy. I'll call you later I have something to tell you. I want to be the one to tell you so that nobody else could let you know.

Me: What is it?

Dex: Don't worry about it, I'm not going to tell you over the phone. You'll find out when I get back to town, just know I'm sorry I didn't know I had to do this.

Me: If it's something you need to tell me, I rather you tell me through text message so that I don't have to see you ever again.

Dex: I said I'm not telling you over the phone and trust me I know once you find out you won't want to have anything to do with me.

Now, I was starting to worry. What kind of trouble did he get himself into and how the fuck were we going to get him out of it?

Sitting the phone down, I just thought about what he had to tell me. It couldn't be anything bad considering he just left fucking town. I swear if this nigga was about to tell me anything like he had a baby or something I would flip the fuck out and make him hate me.

I had a feeling that he was about to ruin my whole night and I couldn't believe that I let myself catch feelings for somebody like him. This was the last thing I thought would happen, "Calm down Bri. You don't even know what he's going to tell you," I said to myself.

Getting under the covers, I laid down on my soft pillow and held it close to my body before closing my eyes. After tossing and turning for what seemed like twenty minutes, I got out of the bed and went back into the living room. I couldn't even sleep because I was worried about what he was going to tell me.

* * *

Later on, that night, I peeled my body off the couch and went into the bedroom so that I could start getting ready for tonight. Sitting in front of my full length mirror, I plugged up my flat iron and started to curl my hair into some big curls.

Once I was finished, I put on some makeup but not too much, I didn't want to look like somebody painted that shit on like the other women out here. They was always walking around here looking like clowns.

Applying some nude lip gloss to my full lips, I got up and went into my closet. Thanks to Dex, I had a closet full of clothes that I hadn't even gotten the chance to wear, grabbing a black mini skirt, a red leather bra and some red Giuseppe Zanotti hells. Putting them on the bed, I went into the restroom and handled my personal hygiene before walking back out and getting dressed.

Once I was fully dressed, I sat on the couch and took a picture before sending it to Dex's phone. I wanted him to see what he would be missing if he fucked up what he had to me.

Shortly afterwards, he started to call, "Hello?" I answered.

"Where you going with that short ass skirt and bra on?"

"Out, it's Kymani's birthday so we turning up," I nonchalantly spoke.

"Not with that on, you need to change."

"You can't tell me what I can and cannot wear what you need to be worried about is what you have to tell me. You better think long and hard before you tell me because if it's something that bad then I will be leaving you alone."

"Chill, okay. You'll know when I get back in town, I don't want to tell you over the phone because that's not something you tell the love of your life over the phone. Just know that it don't change the way I feel about you but you're not going to like it."

"Are you married? Got another girl pregnant? What is it? I don't want to wait until you get back in town to find out what it is you have to tell me? And why didn't you tell me about Winter being pregnant for you?"

He sighed, "Because she lost the baby and I didn't think I needed to say anything. It's not like the baby is here, it was her fault that she lost the baby, and that's why I stopped fucking with her."

"But it didn't stop you from still fucking her."

"That's old news and this don't have nothing to do with Winter. I love you and I will always love you; I want you to remember that," he said before hanging up the phone.

Sitting up, I rolled me two blunts before getting up and leaving the house. Getting into my brand new black Mercedes Benz, I headed to Kymani's place so that I could pick her up. I didn't want her to drive tonight because I knew she was going to be getting lit and the last thing I needed was for her to drink and drive.

I was her designated driver tonight so my limit on drinks were two. I couldn't have no more than that or I wasn't going to be no good for neither of us to make it home and you can't trust nobody to get you home. When I got to her apartment building, I called her phone and she picked up as she was walking out of the house, "Girl, I see you. I'm heading down now," she said and hung up.

Turning up the music, DaBaby's song *Pony* was playing, and I was twerking my ass in the seat. When she got in, she started bobbing her head then she got back out and started shaking her ass, "Yasss bitch, you ready to turn the fuck up."

"You have no idea, I have been waiting for this day for a long time and I'm happy it's finally here. A bitch is finally on her shit and I don't have Mike to worry about ruining this birthday."

"I can't believe you're twenty-one-years-old."

"Me either."

Putting one of the blunts to my mouth, I lit it and took a long drag from it before passing it to her. On the way to the club, we smoked both of the blunts that I rolled, and she was about to put another to her mouth when we pulled up to the club, "Wait on that, we can smoke it in the club," I told her, and we got out of the car.

Looking into the mirror, I applied some more lip gloss and headed to the front of the line. They had all kinds of women complaining and whining but the bouncer still let us right in, it was a good thing I paid for our booth weeks ahead. The club was already packed, and I didn't think they had enough room for all the people that were waiting outside, "Excuse me ma," a deep voice said from behind me while he grabbed my waist.

When he got on the side of me, I looked into his face and for some reason my heart was thumping, and my pussy was pulsating. He was so fucking sexy, and his deep voice did something to me, "You good," I smiled, and he smiled right back.

"Thank you beautiful. Have a good night tonight."

We went up to the section. Winter and Barbie were already sitting down smoking and drinking, "About time!" Winter yelled standing up and hugging Kymani then me.

"Why y'all bitches left Briana's without saying anything?" she asked.

"Because we needed to get our fits for tonight and make sure everything was set up for you to enjoy it."

I plopped down on the couch and Kymani put the blunt to her mouth and lit it. Barbie handed me the blunt she was smoking on and I hit it while watching the dance floor. I hoped that tonight went well and that nobody ruined our night like they always did out there.

*B*riana was bothering me about something that I made clear I didn't want to tell her until I made it back to town. I knew that she was going to hate me when she found out what I had to tell her, "What you gon' do? You know fuck well Briana is not about to settle for this shit." Dreux told me something I already knew.

"I know that shit, I have to figure out what the fuck I'm going to do. I don't want to lose her but man I had to do this to make sure everything went accordingly to plan."

"You did this to take over for your father, I would have told him fuck him."

"I should have, but it was too late. We're going to see more money than we've ever seen before. I just need you to keep this shit from Kymani until I tell Briana, if she finds out she's going to run her mouth."

"I won't say anything, you should already know that. I just want you to know that you fucked up."

"Okay, he gets it and it's not his fault. Your father should have told you what you was going to have to do to take over for him," Isabelle chimed in.

"This some fucked up shit, I feel like I got played and now it ain't shit I could do about it."

"Nope, we have to stay married for about two years before we can get a divorce. I don't want to be married to you either just so you know. I had a good thing going on before this shit happened."

"I'm sorry about that, had I known I wouldn't have even took him up on his offer."

"'My father made the deal for me to marry his first born son and since he got killed, I have to settle for you. I've met Trayvion and I liked him so much, I hope you're something like him."

"When did you meet him?" I asked.

"Weeks before I got the phone call that he got killed. I don't know but I'm starting to think that he didn't want to marry me, so your father had him murdered."

Isabella is my new wife and I couldn't stand her ass. She was a sweet-heart and was doing every and anything that her father told her to do. I guess this is what happens when you're fathered by a big king pin like her father, Roc Gonzales. Yea, I fucked up marrying her, but I didn't have a choice especially if I wanted all control over the organization, but I don't think it's worth me losing Briana in the process.

Getting up from the table, I went out on the balcony of the estate that we were now living in to check my phone. I had Travis go to the club so that I could see what Briana was up to while I wasn't there. She never went to the club without me, but I couldn't think that she was going to stay in the house while I was miles away from her.

Scrolling through the pictures, I spotted one of her and some nigga standing on the side of each other and she was staring int o his eyes like she knew him. Dialing Travis' number, I waited for him to answer and when he did you could hear the music blasting in the background, "Who is that nigga she's standing next to?"

"You ain't gon' believe this but that's Roc's oldest son Grant."

"You mean the one that was adopted. He only have one biological child and that's Isabelle."

"I guess so, you want me to find out who his real people are?" he asked.

"Nah, don't worry about it. I can't be trying to control what she do all they did was exchange some words it don't mean she gon' go home with him."

"You right about that, she's in her section with Kymani, Winter, and Barbie."

"Winter?" I let out a breath. That's why she asked me that shit earlier. Winter trying to get Briana to stop fucking with me and I just gave her the whole reason of why she wasn't going to be with me.

"Yea, it seems like they've become good friends or some shit."

"I doubt it. Winter is probably using Briana to try to get her to stop fucking with me. Thank you," I hung up the phone and went back into the house.

"Everything okay?" Isabella asked.

"Yea, we're going to head back to Texas tomorrow. I have some business I have to handle."

"Okay," she replied.

Leaving her in the kitchen, I went upstairs and into the guest bedroom that I was sleeping in. Laying back on the bed, I shook my head. I had gotten myself into some deep shit and I didn't know how the fuck I was going to get out of it, but I had to think of something.

Roc made it perfectly clear that I had to stay married to his daughter for a certain amount of time before he signed over the organization to me. I was going to make this shit work until then. None of them knew about Briana. The only one that knew about her was Isabelle, and I didn't know how she really felt about me having somebody that I held so dear to me still being in the picture.

I didn't even give a fuck. I had more shit to worry about when I got back to Texas like this meeting. I had to have with some of the other big dope men in the game, so I had to get my head on straight because if I went in there bullshitting, they would feed me to the wolves.

Kymani

*L*ast night was so lit, but it was even better when I went home and Dreux was sitting in the living room on the sofa in nothing but his boxers, "I thought you wasn't coming back until tomorrow?"

"I decided to come back early so that I could give you your birthday present in private."

"And what is it?" I asked cocking my head to the side and looking at his dick that was playing peek a boo. I thought it was so sweet that Dreux came back early to give me my gift. Even if he didn't have one, I still would have been grateful for him.

"This and this," he said pulling a box from behind him and grabbing his dick at the same time. Walking over to him, I kissed his lips and took the box from him. Sitting on the couch I opened the box and looked at the diamond necklace that was sitting so pretty.

"I love it. Thank you," I smiled.

He grabbed the box from me and took the necklace out, putting it on my neck he let it fall and the heart on the front of it was in the middle of my chest, "I want you to wear this all the time so that you could know how I feel about you. We haven't been together for long and I'm not ready to say the I love you words to you just yet, but at least you know a nigga really feeling you."

"I know you are and that's why I was turning niggas down left and right tonight."

"Oh yea? I knew I shouldn't have left until after your birthday."

"Why? So you can shoot somebody for hitting on me."

"Damn right, you're mine and that's the way it's going to always be. Don't let me being out of town fool you. I'll always come back to you."

"Mhm, I bet you will. Is Dex back with you?"

"No, he'll be back tomorrow. We have some meetings to attend to when he gets here so don't even tell Briana that he's back."

"Why? What's going on between them two?"

"I'm not saying anything, you'll find out sooner or later until then keep what I just told you to yourself," he said and got up from the couch.

Leaning down, he picked me up and carried me into the bedroom. Throwing me in the middle of the bed, he started to take his clothes off and I did the same, it was one way I wanted to be fucked tonight and that was from the back. I was drunk and needed him to pound this shit out of me.

Once I was completely naked, I turned over and arched my back so that he could get to work. I felt his dick sliding up and down my pussy then he went down and sucked on my shit from the back making me run a lil' bit. "Don't run from it," he told me before pulling me back and sliding his tongue deep inside of me.

I twerked and threw my pussy on his tongue until I couldn't anymore, putting my hand on my clit I started to rub on it. "Mm. Oh shit," I let out.

WHAP!

He slapped both of my ass cheeks while still eating me from the back, "Fuck," I whined.

"You want this dick?" he asked, and I nodded my head. He got off the bed and moved me back until my legs were hanging off the side of the bed. He slapped his long dick on my ass a few times before sliding inside of me with no warning.

"Shitttttt," I moaned while grabbing and gripping the side of the bed. I was tearing the sheets off the bed and my pillows were moving down to where I was that's how hard he was fucking me. "Oh my god, wait!"

He moved back and I adjusted myself so that I wouldn't fall off the bed. Reaching my hand behind me, I grabbed his waist and pulled him back to me. He slid his dick back inside of me and went so deep that I laid down on my stomach. He then laid on top of me and started pounding in and out of me like he had a point to prove.

I was gasping for air with each stroke he delivered to me, "Ahh."

"Damn, I missed you and I haven't been gone that long."

"I miss you too daddy!" I screamed when he pushed deeper inside of me.

Leaning down, he wrapped his arms around my waist and picked me up. Still inside of me, he went to the full-length mirror that was hanging on the back of my door and bounced me up and down on his dick, "Damn, fuck," he groaned in my ear, "I like watching my dick slide in and out of you. Open your eyes."

Opening my eyes, I couldn't believe the sight of his massive dick inside of me. He raised me up even higher and slammed me down making my juices immediately drip down. I was squirting all over the mirror and his dick.

"I can't, oh my god. It hurts," I told him.

"Just a lil' while longer, it feels so good," he whispered in my ear.

Walking back over to the bed, he pulled me off his dick and pushed me on my back. Putting my legs over his shoulders, he grabbed himself and slid right back inside of me, "Ooh."

I started to fuck him back and the only sounds that you could hear throughout the whole house was my breathing and moaning and our bodies slapping against each other. It was getting hot and I needed to cut the air on before I sweated my hair out which was already happening.

"Take this dick."

"I'm about to cum!" I moaned out as loud as I could.

"Me too," he growled in my ear before pushing himself deeper inside and me and letting his seeds go.

When we finished, I got up and went into the restroom so that I could take a shower. After that sex session this is exactly what I needed. Turning the hot water on, I waited for it to get as hot as it could and was about to step in when somebody started knocking on the front door.

"Who is that?" Dreux asked putting his clothes on in a hurry.

"I don't know, are you expecting anybody?" I asked putting my robe on and walking out of the bedroom and to the door.

Looking through the peephole, I saw that it was Mike, Dreezy, and Quez, and they were all holding boxes in their hands, "What are y'all doing here?" I asked never opening the door.

"You think I was going to forget your birthday. I know we're not together, but I still want you to have this," Mike responded and Dreux moved me back and opened the door.

"She don't need your gifts," he told him.

"I'm not trying to disrespect you, I brought these while we were still together and was going to give them to her on her birthday, but I didn't know we weren't going to be together," I heard Mike tell him.

Dreux cracked the door and looked at me, "Do you want the gifts?" he asked.

"I mean if he wants me to have them, I'll take them," I answered.

He walked away from the door and I stood there and grabbed the boxes from them, "Thank you," I told him with a semi smile on my face.

"No problem. Enjoy your night," he said and they all walked away from the door. Shutting it behind them, I turned around and Dreux was sitting on the couch with an attitude.

"Before you even think anything, I didn't know he knew where I stayed."

"How do he know where you stay? He's so comfortable with knocking on your front door."

"It's nothing like you're thinking. I haven't talked to Mike since the day I saw him with Jazz at the nail salon."

"I believe you, but you shouldn't have taken the gifts, now he's going to think that he has a chance at getting you back."

"I don't care for materialistic things, what I care about is honesty and loyalty which Mike didn't have to give to me. He didn't know how to be any of those things, and I should have been left him alone, but I couldn't because my dumb ass thought I was in love with him."

"And now?"

"Now, he doesn't have a chance to get back with me. I know you don't trust him, but you have to trust me. I'm not interested in being with Mike ever again, my mind is set on you."

"Good, because I wasn't going to give you up without a fight anyway," he chuckled and pulled me down on the couch next to him. We sat there and held each other for moment before he sighed and got up, "I have to head out, don't open the door for anybody if it ain't me."

"I don't even have to open the door for you because it looks like you have your own key."

"I may have the hook up with the lady in the front office."

"I'ma get on her ass for giving you a key without checking with me. You could have been a serial killer or rapist and she just gave you a key to my apartment."

"I told her you was my wife," he smiled and walked out of the door.

Getting up, I locked it behind him then leaned my head on the back of it and smiled. He got on my damn nerves, but I liked him so much. Heading back into the bedroom, I stripped my covers and sheets off the bed and put some other ones on it, before getting into the shower.

Standing close to the water, I hurriedly grabbed a towel and some shower gel and started to scrub my body until I felt clean enough. Getting out, I wrapped a black towel around my breast and walked out of the restroom. Sitting on the floor I cleaned my mirror then rolled me a blunt so that I could smoke and relax before getting in the bed and opening these gifts that Mike got for me.

I had to admit, it felt good that he still thought about me enough to bring me my gifts and it was creepy that he knew where I stayed and that told me one thing and that was, he followed me home one day. Once the mirror was squeaky clean, I put the blunt to my mouth and lit it.

Taking a long drag from it, I unwrapped the first gift and smiled looking at the Dolce and Gabbana black clutch. Sitting that one to the side, I opened the next one and it was a diamond studded bracelet that had my name spelled out in diamonds. He went all out I see, grabbing the last one which was a card, I opened it and read what the card said then grabbed the one-thousand-dollars out of it and put it into the clutch that he gotten me.

Picking up the trash, I walked out of the room and put it in the trash can before going back into the bedroom. I hid the other gifts in the back of my closet then got into the bed.

When I finished the blunt, I laid under the covers and rolled over my side. Looking into the dark space, my eyes started to get heavy, flipping on my other side I said a silent prayer and went to bed.

Mike

hen that nigga Dreux opened that door, I wanted to punch him in the face and just stomp him the fuck out, but I didn't want Kymani to hate me more than she already did. "You good? I know it can't be easy knowing that your ex girl that you in love with is giving away what should be yours?" Dreezy asked.

"It's not but what the fuck can I do about it, I fucked up when I got Jazz pregnant. I don't regret my son at all but, I'm starting to think that he was supposed to be a product of me and Kymani's love not me and Jazz."

"That's how it goes sometimes, you can't control who you have kids with. Yo' ass should have never been fucking over Kymani anyway. She's a good woman and you fucked that up all for a status in these streets!" Quez spat.

"Nigga, you don't think I know that shit? I lost my girl to a light skinned Chris Brown look alike and it ain't shit I can do about it. She deserves to be happy even if it's not with me, so if y'all niggas don't mind I don't want to talk about this shit no more," I told them before taking a long drag from the blunt and passing it around.

We were sitting on the porch of our brand new trap house and shit was going good on this end. I may not have had Kymani to share all this shit with, but I seeing more money than half these niggas that's been slanging all their lives. I also managed to get in good with Dex, all it took was a phone call and me telling him that I would leave Kymani alone.

"Do you think this truce with Dex and Dreux going to last?" Dreezy asked.

"As long as I stay away from Kymani and Briana, it should. They don't want me to have anything to do with either of them. They also want us to transfer some drugs."

"To where?"

"I'll let y'all know when I find out."

"You think it's a good idea to be transporting for these niggas, how we know it's not a set up to get us locked up or some shit?" Quez asked.

"I'm with Quez on this one, I don't trust them niggas or they word for a second. You can transport them drugs by yourself and we'll make sure you're straight when you get locked up. They want you out of the picture and without you they think we won't be able to sell."

"Well, they have their facts all wrong. If I ever get caught up, I want y'all to keep doing what y'all doing and make sure my son and Jazz straight."

"You tripping for even considering doing that shit."

"I don't have a choice, if I don't do this then they try everything in their power to get us knocked off the map then we ain't gon' be able to sell nowhere."

"I would rather get a regular job then become a mule for them niggas. I really thought you had a mind of your own."

"Fuck you mean? I do, but I'm doing what I have to do for my family,.

See you niggas would never understand because y'all don't have families to look after. Y'all do this shit because it's something to do, I do this because this is how I make my living."

"I feel you on that shit, but at the same time I don't understand it. You do what you have to do and I'm going to hold down the fort if anything happens to you."

"That's all I ask," I dapped them both up then jumped off the porch and went to my car. Unlocking the door, I hopped inside and backed out of the driveway, so that I could go home and get ready for this date night shit that Jazz had me participating in every weekend.

She was lucky that I was really starting to get feelings for her, because if I wasn't ain't no way I would be doing this shit.

$\mathcal{J}$he next morning, I woke up and my body was sore as fuck. Rolling out of the bed, I went into the bathroom and handled my personal hygiene before heading out to Kymani's place. Her birthday may have been last night, but we was celebrating the whole weekend. I wanted her to have a birthday that she would always remember and then we was going to do the same when my birthday rolled around next month.

When I was finished, I walked out and got dressed in some black ripped jeans, a white plain v neck, and on my feet were some black and white Vans. Putting my hair up into a ponytail, I headed for the door when somebody started banging on it like they were the police.

"Who the fuck is it?" I asked.

"Open the door hoe," Kymani's voice replied.

Moving back, I unlocked the door and let her inside, "I was coming to your house remember?"

"I know, but I couldn't wait any longer for your ass."

"Hmm, that's a cute necklace," I admired the heart studded diamond necklace that was around her neck.

"Thank you, it's a gift from Dreux."

"He's back in town?" I asked.

"Yea, he came back to surprise me. Have you heard from Dex?"

"No, which is funny because if Dreux is back that mean he's back."

"He is, I'm not supposed to say anything because Dex wanted to surprise you but we both knew I couldn't hide this from you."

"I'm not understanding why he didn't come over last night or call me to let me know he was back out here. Something don't seem right with this and I bet it has something to do with what he has to tell me."

"What you talking about?" she asked.

"I'm talking about the fact that Dex texted me talking about he had something to tell me and that I was going to probably hate him once he did."

"I wonder what the fuck that is, why would he tell you that over a text then not tell you what it is. You don't think he went to New York and got somebody pregnant that fast?"

"If so, his ass was busy and that would explain why I barely saw him when we was out there. I swear if he bring his ass here talking about, he have a baby on the way I'm going to lose it and stab his bitch ass," I snapped.

"Well, let's not jump to conclusions. I don't think Dex is that stupid to fuck over you like that."

"You'd be surprised. It don't even seem like a shock to me. I mean he didn't even feel the need to tell me about Winter being pregnant and he lied about how serious they were in the first place."

"I feel you on that part right there, he should have told you about them even if you didn't want to hear it."

"Exactly, I'm not worried about it. If I wasn't the first thing on his mind with him being back, then I'm not about to be sitting here worried about him. He knows where to find me if he want to see me." And with that, I grabbed my bag and car keys and we walked out of the house.

Getting into the car, I pulled out of the spot and made my way to a restaurant that Kymani loved to go to when we were out here. The only thing that was on my mind was making sure that my friend had a good time for her birthday since last year Mike ruined the whole party with his controlling. We couldn't do nothing, drink, smoke, or dance, because he was so scared that somebody was going to be trying to hit on Kymani.

We ended up just saying fuck the club and going back to her place and watching movies and smoking two deep.

When we got to the restaurant, we got out and went inside. After getting seated, my phone started to ring, and it was Dex. Hitting the ignore button, I was about to put it back into my purse when he started calling again and yet again, I hit the ignore button. He was about to learn not to fuck with me.

If I wasn't on your mind, then you wasn't on mine and that was the way I was going to have to start treating that nigga because he had me twisted. I never held back my feelings for Dex but I'm happy I didn't tell him I loved him because I had a feeling in my soul that he was about to fuck up my happiness and his all for the dope game.

If that's what he wanted to do, then he was going to have to blow my phone up or pop up at my house to tell me whatever it was that he had to say.

"Hi, I'm Bryana and I'm going to be serving you today. What kind of drink can I start y'all off with?" she asked with a smile on her face.

"I'll have a mimosa and she'll have the same," I ordered for us both.

Kymani was all in her phone that she didn't even hear what I said, "I'll have a mimosa," she finally spoke up.

Me and the server started to laugh, and she looked at us both, "She already ordered that for you. Do y'all need a minute to look at the menu?" she asked.

"Yes please."

Nodding her head, she walked away, and I looked around the restaurant until I spotted Winter and Barbie walking inside with some of the other dancers from the club. When they came to our table, I looked up at them and smiled, "Are you still the boss even if Dex is back?"

"Yea, why what's up?"

"The new manager y'all hired is an ass," Winter told me.

"What you mean?"

"I mean, he's trying to take fifty-percent of our earnings and he's been pocketing them."

"I'll talk to Dex and let him know so that we can handle that. In the meantime, what are y'all about to get into?"

"We're headed to this private party that Dex wants us to do."

I was confused. I was still trying to figure out why the hell he didn't tell me about this shit. I mean if I'm the boss of the club then he needed to run this kind of shit by me but that's probably why he was calling too.

"Don't worry, we'll be back at the club tonight," she said, and they walked about away from the table and out of the door.

"Do you want to follow them and see where they going?"

"I don't know, that seems stalkerish. I just don't understand why he didn't feel the need to tell me about this shit."

"Your phone rang twice, and you hit the ignore button. I'm guessing that was him."

"Yea, but I didn't answer because I was busy," I lied.

"Briana, you have to show some professionalism. He left you in charge therefore he has to call and let you know about him borrowing the dancers. Call him and see what he wanted and stop acting like a brat."

Rolling my eyes, I pulled my phone out of my purse and unlocked it. Sliding his number to the left, I put it to my ear and waited for him to answer. "Yo?" his deep voice spoke.

"You called?"

"Yea, I was calling to tell you that I needed to use the dancers for a private event."

"And am I invited to this private event?" I asked and he sighed.

"It's men only, but I'll come to the crib so that we could talk."

"Dex…" a woman's voice called out.

"Don't worry about it," I said and hung up the phone. Putting it back into my purse, I sipped on my drink and waited for the server to come back with our food. When she did, she sat the plates in front of us then walked away.

"Are you okay?" Kymani asked.

"I'm fine, he said that the party was men only, but I heard a woman saying his name in the background."

"I say let's pull up and get the answers we need."

"You don't have to do that, this is my issue."

"Oh, I do because if he is there then nine times out of ten Dreux is too and if so, I want to catch him in the act so I can bust him upside his head."

"I don't know, I just don't think I will get much out of it."

"I'll tell you what, if he's hiding something then I'm pretty sure we can find out at that private event. The only restaurant that does private events is the one that's called Player's Room which is for all the big dope boys that's in the game or coming into the game."

I had no clue what she was talking about, but I wanted to go. "How are we even going to get in?"

"Honey, we're dating two men that's been on the scene for a long time. I'm betting that one of us should be able to use our man's name to get inside."

"Let's go."

Getting up, I threw two hundred dollars on the table to pay for the food then we left. Climbing back into my car, I pulled out of the parking lot and headed to this club. When we got there it was so packed. The doors were semi opened and one of the bouncers from the club was standing there.

"I have an idea. We won't have to use either of them nigga's names because Bo is at the door and we both know he has a thing for me."

"And me," Kymani spoke, and we laughed.

Bo swears he was a player and he was if you wanted to get into the club, he was the man you had to talk to or flirt with. I've done that so many times when I wasn't even supposed to be going in clubs.

Stepping out of the car, we walked up to the door and Bo stood up and pulled both me and Kymani into his embrace, "What you doing here shorty?" he asked.

"trying to see what my dancers up to."

"You know your man is in there with some female on his side."

"Oh yea, I didn't even know he was going to be attending."

"I'll let you in so that you can handle your business. Just don't start nothing, this club is for the elite men of the streets only and I can't have you in there acting a fool."

"You don't have to worry about that Bo," I patted him on his chest and walked into the building.

When we got inside, I looked around and spotted Dex sitting in a booth with a female all over him and one of the strippers on his lap. He was laughing and talking, having a funky good time and I couldn't wait till he saw my face and fucked up that whole moment.

"Just chill for a lil' while longer," Kymani told me.

Nodding my head, I pulled a blunt out of my purse and put it to my mouth. "Need a light?" one of the strippers asked putting one to the blunt.

"Thanks."

"I know you're only here to keep an eye on your old man and that's fine. I won't say anything about that, but that girl next to him is more than just a business associate, they've been kissing, and I don't mean on the cheek kissing," she let me know.

"Thank you for letting me know Spencer," I told her before sliding a hundred-dollar bill in her thongs. I had to make it look like I was there for the party as well before getting up and shutting Dex's fun down.

"I can't believe this nigga is playing you, you're the baddest bitch in this place," Kymani boosted my confidence.

"Girl, he's going to find out what it feels like to have his heart played with. I'm about to show him right now," I smirked and knocked back the shot that was sitting in front of me. Getting up, I stripped out of my clothes and started walking around the party.

"What's up sexy? Come sit on daddy's lap," a sexy older Mexican man with a strong accent spoke.

Slowly walking over to him, I sat in his lap and started twerking my ass to the song that was on. His old ass couldn't even keep up with me, he kept letting me slip off his lap with his fat ass.

Standing up in front of him, I bent over and started shaking my ass in his face and him and a few dudes that was around him started making it rain on me and I'm not talking dollar bills but hundred dollar bills. "Damn, she thick as fuck," I heard Dex say.

Raising up, I looked into his eyes and smiled at him. Watching that smile on his face disappear into a mug made me laugh. I walked closer to Dex and stood on my tippy toes, "Enjoy the rest of your party," I whispered in his ear before pushing passed him.

"Nah, bring yo' ass here," he snapped grabbing my arm and pulling me back to him.

"Dex, is something wrong?" a female asked walking up on him. She put her hand on his and I saw a big ass rock on her ring finger.

"Who is this? The bitch you been cheating on me with?"

"No, sweetie, I'm his wife…"

To Be Continued…

ABOUT THE AUTHOR

 I am twenty-six year old Urban Fiction author Vee Bryant. Born and raised in Texas. Reading has been a passion of mine since I was a child. I used to write a lot of short stories that made me fall in love with writing. I have two kids, one living and one dead. both girls. They're the reason I work so hard. My debut series with Royalty is called All I Need In This Life of Sin Is A Thug's Love and it's a three-part series. I have a full catalog if you would like to indulge in my crazy characters and storylines.

I have written 16 novels in the last seven months and not stopping anytime soon. I have a wild imagination and want to take my readers on this journey with me.

 facebook.com/LilTrill34

Royalty Publishing House is now accepting manuscripts from aspiring or experienced urban romance authors!

WHAT MAY PLACE YOU ABOVE THE REST:

Heroes who are the ultimate book bae: strong-willed, maybe a little rough around the edges but willing to risk it all for the woman he loves.

Heroines who are the ultimate match: the girl next door type, not perfect - has her faults but is still a decent person. One who is willing to risk it all for the man she loves.

The rest is up to you! Just be creative, think out of the box, keep it sexy and intriguing!

If you'd like to join the Royal family, send us the first 15K words (60 pages) of your completed manuscript to submissions@royaltypublish-inghouse.com

LIKE OUR PAGE!

Be sure to <u>LIKE</u> our Royalty Publishing House page on Facebook!

CPSIA information can be obtained
at www.ICGtesting.com
Printed in the USA
BVHW031338190619
551432BV00001B/48/P

9 781072 816904